Too Sweet

A Highschool Vampire Romance

Monroe Wildrose

Contents

Trigger Warning List:

- Heavy Language

- Teenage Smoking

- Depiction of a Type 1 Diabetic Character (Injections, needles, and medication use)

- Bullying (Mild)

- The suggestion of child abuse (Off page)

- Kidnapping

- Hostage situation

- Mention of Blood (Heavy)

- Stabbing

Dedicated to all those battling Type 1 Diabetes.
You are not a burden.

Chapter One

Briar

The thing about high school is that it is complete bullshit.

I wouldn't recommend saying that to your advanced mathematics teacher in the middle of his class, unless you wanted to be sent to the principal's office.

Or you could anyway, knowing you were going to be staring down Mrs. Sheridan's stony eyes. The woman had a stare like a loaded shotgun.

She wasn't even the principal, oh no. This was my counselor. The woman I saw after I saw the principal. Usually, they would call my parents for this meeting. However, my mother worked just shy of an hour away at a bar she owned in the bigger city outside this piece of shit town and wouldn't come anyway.

Not in a neglectful way. It's just my mother also thought high school was bullshit. That, and I was always getting in trouble. Not real trouble. Not drugs or house party trouble, just questioning authority trouble. My mother admired it in me, coaxed it, and encouraged the flame of her child's unruly behavior until it was a wildfire that consumed all adults I came into contact with.

"Briar," Mrs. Sheridan sighed.

It wasn't her fault I was in here so often. So often, the counselor stocked my favorite vanilla-flavored tootsie rolls in a little glass candy jar on her desk. My hand was caught fishing in the pot when she said my name, and my eyes slid to hers.

"Briar, you can't talk back to your teachers."

"Why not?" I pulled two light blue candies out and replaced the metal lid.

"I can't have this conversation with you every time."

"Mr. Gornheld is an idiot, and he told me I couldn't drink a juicebox in class."

"Were you drinking juice because your sugar was low, or just because you wanted one?"

"Since I have sworn never to lie to you, Jackie, I'm afraid I can't answer that."

Mrs. Sheridan, a.k.a. Jackie, gave me the shotgun eyes again. At one time, I thought the stare was more intimidating. I still found it slightly scary, but I was proud to say my face would never register that.

"Please don't call me Jackie."

I nodded, chewing the slightly hard candy.

"Despite your opinions on Mr. Gornheld, you cannot call him an idiotic twit in the middle of class."

"Is it derailing my behavior map?"

"There is no *behavior map*; I'm just concerned these outbursts are a sign of something deeper than you thinking the adults at this school are incompetent," she corrected me. "Only halfway through senior year, Briar."

"Not you, Mrs. Sheridan; you aren't."

"High praise." She nearly rolled her eyes, and I smiled as she stopped herself. "I saw your locker this morning."

"You'd think they'd get more creative over time, but it seems the blood that their brain should be using is being redirected."

Whore. Bitch.

Two words painted in rose gold spray-paint on my locker. It wasn't the first time and probably wouldn't be the last. I would go to the admin office and ask for some paint thinner and a mask to remove the words after my classes had finished. Of course, the custodian would do it for me if I left it, but there was a specific power in angrily wiping away the letters while wearing a fume mask as kids shuffled past me to go home.

"You want to talk about it?" she asked as I contemplated grabbing another tootsie roll.

"Maybe if I cared."

"You flinched when I brought it up."

Okay, so I cared. So what. I didn't care about the boys who painted it. I didn't care one second about them and their stupid ideas of humor and brotherly devotion. I did care a little about who they did it on behalf of.

Morgan.

Morgan Pope. My Ex.

Ex seemed like such a dramatic word. We were only seventeen, so what if we had been together for two years? So what if I had fallen so hopelessly and terribly in love with him that I thought there was no way that we wouldn't be together forever? Until we weren't, and when he broke up with me over the summer, rumors started flying in this piece of shit place. Rumors that he broke up with me because I was a lousy lay. I had been...a little distressed.

No one was there to witness me cry myself to sleep for a week. And if no one was there to see, then it never happened.

"You know he didn't break up with me because I was bad in bed," I said absently, remembering how the first time the words had left Kelly Hilden's pink pouty mouth, I had nearly decked her.

"Who?" Mrs. Sheridan asked, and I narrowed my eyes at her.

She knew who. Everyone in the school knew.

Because Morgan Pope wasn't just a bad boy, he was *the* bad boy in Ironside High. The bad boy who had picked me of all the girls that were dripping off his toned arms. With his midnight hair and dark brown eyes, he was everything a high school girl could dream of.

And he had dated me. A five foot eight, thick girl who had to wiggle herself into a size fourteen jeans. Not that he ever made me feel bad about that. I didn't feel bad about that; I loved my thick thighs... kind of wished my boobs were more prominent, but what seventeen-year-old girl didn't?

"I didn't sleep with him at all, and he said that after two years of dating, if I didn't want to sleep with him, then we should break up."

"Hm," she responded.

"He's not a bad guy, Morgan; he just...was tired of waiting for me to commit."

"I'm proud of you for not letting yourself be pressured. Having sex for the first time is personal, and you should be very comfortable with the person."

"I was comfortable with Morgan...," I defended him, but if I was comfortable with him, why had I chosen to break up rather than be intimate?

He was patient and never pressured me. Until the end, and even then, it wasn't like he had gotten angry. He just seemed sad.

"Is it Morgan doing that to your locker?" she asked.

"No," I said quickly. Too quickly. "It's his dumb friends."

I was spilling my guts, when I prided myself on my stoic countenance. Luckily Mrs. Sheridan had some sort of confidentiality code she couldn't break unless a student was showing concerning signs of un-aliving themselves, or if they were violent in some form.

I was neither of those things. Just a repeat offender that Mrs. Sheridan would have to deal with until the end of the year, then I would be out of her hair for good. I hoped she had a quiet following year after I was gone, with only minimally challenging kids. She deserved it.

"Well, can I be on my way Jackie?" I asked, slapping my thighs.

"Yes, please refrain from yelling at, cussing out, or name-calling the teachers in this school." She waved me out.

"Until next time." I gave her a ceremonious bow.

Since advanced math was my last class of the day, I headed to the admin office for them to call the custodian to give me my cleaning supplies.

I waited in an uncomfortable chair inside the office for Anthony to bring me the goods while listening to kids pouring out of every door. For a the hours of freedom, they were like addicts.

I picked at my maroon Doc Martens, which had one sole coming off. It would be time to retire them soon. My mom would oblige me if I asked for new ones, but I liked to wear things all the way down before replacing them.

Someone walked into the office, and I gave them a passing glance before returning my gaze to my shoes and the black lace tights, which had miraculously not ripped during the day.

"Darcy Booker." I heard Susan, the admin lady, say. *Sorry, Ms. Diaz, not Susan.*

Darcy Booker was a tall basketball player. Tall wasn't the right word. At nearly eighteen years old, this kid must have been six-four or six-five. I had seen this lanky gargantuan palm a basketball in the gym. Besides his height and hand size, the kid's personality was soft like a Georgia peach, and he was as sweet as the pies people made from them.

The school was so small that everyone knew everyone, and when Darcy had transferred here at the beginning of the school year, he, and his brother Crispin, were quick to get noticed.

Darcy was fair with freckles across his face, ears that stuck out just a bit, and a slightly crooked nose that I assumed he broke playing some sport. His eyes were pretty...for a jock kid—the green-blue color of that fake sea glass they sold in touristy coastal towns.

When I heard Anthony's cart rolling up, Darcy was chatting with Ms. Diaz about some grade transfer or something. I pushed myself out of my seat as Anthony walked in with the rags, mask, and paint thinner already in hand.

"You know I will do that for you," he reminded me, but I just nodded and took the stuff from him.

I turned after he left because the office had gone silent. Ms. Diaz was no longer at the counter, and Darcy was staring at me. His stare was open, even as I caught him, as if he didn't care if I found him out.

"What are you looking at?" I sneered at him, and a wide grin split his face.

"You." His answer came as sure as his stare and I was speechless for about five seconds. How dare he stare at me and then have the audacity to tell me he was staring at me.

"You should take a picture; it will last longer." I rolled my eyes and turned.

"If I did, would you autograph it for me?"

As I left the office, I stuffed the rags under my arm with a middle finger raised behind me.

Chapter Two

Briar

My insulin pump beeped at me loudly for the third time. I hit the button on the side to silence it, and five minutes later, my phone alarm, which was hooked to my sensor, started going off. I slid it out of my back pocket and narrowed my eyes at the screen that said my sugar was going high. The little arrow was pointing directly up.

I took my pump off where it was clipped to my waistband. I should have checked my sugar manually, but felt too lazy. Giving myself insulin to correct the number on the screen I clipped the pump back on my pants and setting my phone on the counter, went back to stirring my alfredo sauce.

I resisted the urge to add more freshly grated parmesan, bought from one of those fancy natural grocery places on the way home from school. I pulled the baked chicken out of the oven and let it rest.

Mom ate a lot of bar food. It just came with the job. Not that there was anything wrong with a greasy hamburger or some chili cheese fries, but I liked her to eat something nice a couple of times a week. So, I had been taking online culinary classes that I had asked for as a gift for Christmas last year. I hadn't learned anything crazy, but my understanding of the ingredients and tools had improved.

Once I plated the pasta, I slid the sliced chicken on top with a sprinkle of chopped parsley. I made my mom's plate and covered it in the fridge before eating alone at the kitchen table, reading the comics from the Sunday paper my mom always picked up.

It was sometimes nice to eat alone. Sometimes it was not nice at all. I felt like I had been eating dinner alone since I was seven, getting off the bus, and heading to this apartment. But I would never complain.

My father left my mom when I was five, a year after I had been diagnosed with type one, leaving my mom to navigate having an elementary school kid with an autoimmune disorder on her own.

There were so many things that had to happen, and the two hardest things were getting five-year-old me to take insulin shots with every meal and right before bed. Not to mention the financial strain it put on my mom, a self-employed woman. Private healthcare costs were one thing, but the copays, the co-insurance, the maximums, not to mention the insurance constantly changing the terms of what they would cover all the time, might have sent my mom into an early grave. It might have, if she didn't have an obstinate only child who liked to lie about how much food she had eaten.

My mom was my hero in the cheesiest, most third-grade show-and-tell way possible.

What about my dad, you might ask? Well, he was a well-paid employee of a timeshare company who had found a woman eight years my mother's junior, married her, and was living his best life with his two new kids. He'd signed over any parental rights and now thought it appropriate to invite me to holiday meals with the new family whenever it struck his fancy. Like I was an old Chevy Stepside, someone brought to a car show once a quarter and then put in their garage the rest of the time. I was the retro model only brought out at Christmas.

His wife was lovely; Nancy was her name, and it wasn't like she was a wicked witch or anything. I think she felt as awkward as I did at those rare dinners when I accepted my dad's invitations. Their kids Gunnar and Zoe were also pretty cute but much younger than me. I guess they were my half-siblings though I didn't think of them like that—just little kids of a woman I didn't hate and a man I kind of did.

But I had everything I needed.

I had a mom that loved me. I got good grades. I was currently boyfriend-less, but that wasn't important, no matter how I felt about it now.

I shook off the thoughts in favor of some more mind-numbing, and regular teenage life.

I did some homework and watched reruns of Supernatural until I was so tired that I couldn't keep my eyes open. I slipped into new underwear and a tank top and fell into bed.

On my nightstand, there was a picture of me and Triana, my best friend. We had gone to the same elementary and middle schools together but different high schools. It had been hard for us to adjust, but she came over at least once a week. We mostly just did homework together and helped each other when we could.

She was short with a thick head of cropped brown hair and wore wire frame glasses. I towered over her, and I was only five foot eight.

Next to that picture was one of Morgan and me on our second date. He took it with one of those Polaroid cameras and then bought me a small frame. He had pulled me tight against his chest; his arm reached out with the camera, a sly smile on his face. It contrasted with the smile I wore, which was full and wide, as if I didn't have a care in the world.

I flipped the picture down, pulled the lamp's cord, and rolled over to sleep.

The following day, I sifted through rumpled clothes to find my favorite red shirt with a flying saucer on it that said 'what up, humans'. I pulled on some fishnets and jean shorts. Looking in the mirror, I groaned, realizing already my hair would not cooperate. I tied the burgundy box-dyed waves up in two buns on either side of my head, attacked it with hairspray, and moved on with my day.

I pulled on some frowny-face knee-high socks and my rain-slicker yellow Doc Martens that I saved for special occasions, and hustled into the kitchen. Grabbing the lunch I packed for myself, I reheated some coffee, that was now a day old, and slammed it like I was taking shots at a nightclub.

The kiss I placed on my mother's sleeping forehead was acknowledged with a grunt that meant she loved me. I locked the door behind me and made my way down to the beat-up 2000 black Honda Accord I bought with money I earned from two summer serving jobs and the five hundred my mom matched of that.

Did it smell like smoke from a previous owner? Yes. Did it leak a quart of oil a month? Also, yes. But her name was Evangeline, and she was mine, and no one would take her from me. I put the stick shift into reverse as the seven thousand pine-scented air fresheners swung back and forth from my rearview mirror.

On the way, I listened to an audiobook recording of Jane Eyre that we had to read for English. I was not too fond of it. Jane was too... something. Docile? Level headed? I don't know what it was, but I wanted her to slap Mr. Rochester across the face at almost every turn.

When I got to my locker inside the school, I stared at a freshly painted, artistically depicted male reproductive organ. It had been sprayed with yellow spray paint. *They were getting fancy with it now*; I thought as I put in my combination and set my bag inside.

The principal knew who was spraying my locker. There were security cameras in every hallway of this school. The problem was that the students would be suspended if he came forward with the names. The people in Ironside were a close-knit bunch, and no doubt the parents of the students who would end up getting in trouble would reign hell fire upon our principal's ass. So I understood why he allowed it to happen. I had no respect for him, but I understood.

"Morning, Grey," Roger said from behind me, and I let out a long sigh.

I closed my locker and tried to walk past him without saying anything, but he stepped in my way. A few people filed past us as the halls grew more crowded, but no one paid enough attention to try and help me. Roger was a good friend of Morgan's, and at one time, we had been on okay terms.

"I said, good morning."

"I heard you," I said, staring directly into his eyes. If anyone had a short boy complex, Roger did.

"Not polite not to respond. Not very ladylike."

I wanted to spit in his face. But how early should I send myself to Mrs. Sheridan's office?

"What do you want, Roger?"

"I want you to say good morning."

"Get fucked?" I tried pushing past him, but he blocked me again. "I like the paint you used today; I'm more of a purple girl myself; just tips for next time."

"I don't know what you are talking about." He smiled and swept his auburn hair back off his face.

"You have the paint on your fingers, genius. I am curious, though, are your testicles that large compared to your...you know? Did you pull inspiration directly from yourself? Because, if so, I would see a doctor."

"Smart mouth for an ugly fat girl."

"Stupid mouth for a short man with enlarged balls and a tiny carrot penis."

"You stupid bitch...."

"Roger, let her be."

His voice came to me, and I closed my eyes for a second while swallowing hard. I saw him coming toward us, with Magnolia following right behind him. He looked sloppy as always with his dark hair tied back, but somehow it just dripped sex appeal.

"Let her go to class and stop spraying her locker," Morgan warned now that he was standing in front of us, and I was looking anywhere except his stupidly handsome face.

Roger stepped away. He wouldn't argue with Morgan directly. He might continue to harass me, but he wouldn't do it in front of him. I stepped forward to go to my classes.

"Briar," Morgan called to me.

I stopped like an idiot. Like his word was my pleasure to obey. I hated myself for freezing, but I couldn't move.

"Hey, Magnolia, Roger, I'll catch up with you later?" And with that, the coolest guy in Ironside High dismissed them, and they walked down the hallway to their classes.

Magnolia was nice. Morgan's new girlfriend. I wished she was ugly on the inside so I could hate her, but she was quite lovely. She had long honey hair and freckles with big brown eyes. She was thin, athletic, always polished, and put together. I wanted to dislike her, but there was nothing to hate.

"What?" I found my voice enough to ask.

"How are you doing?" he asked after a moment.

"Great, Morgan, I'm doing great. Is this why you cornered me like this? To ask how I'm doing? Maybe we can get chai lattes after school, and I can open up in a hipster coffeehouse."

"Geez, Briar, relax." He stepped in front of me a bit.

"Make sure Roger stops tagging my locker."

"I'm sorry about that."

"Yeah, I'm sure you are. So sorry that it just keeps happening."

He didn't move but turned and looked at something else to our left. He didn't even have the courtesy to look at me when I lost my mind.

"Why is Booker waving at you?" he asked. His tone was dark, and I recognized it as the possessive jealousy he had when we were together.

"What?" I turned a little and saw that Darcy Booker was looking right at me with a big dopey grin on his face waving his hand at me like I was a plane he was trying to flag down.

"Why. Is. Darcy. Booker. Waving. At. You?" He punctuated each word heavily, demanding an answer.

For some stupid reason, I liked seeing him so pissed off that someone else was waving to me. I wanted to hear that jealousy in his tone. I even liked the way he thought I owed him an explanation.

So, I did another stupid thing to answer my stupid feelings. I raised my hand plastered on a big grin and waved back to Darcy, who looked like I had just gifted him the moon.

"Because we're dating." I didn't look back to see his face, only winked to Darcy as I passed and made my way to my first class.

Chapter Three

Darcy

I was shocked to find out that Briar Grey and I were dating.

Not because I didn't find her admirable or attractive, but because the previous day, she had looked at me in the admin office like I was dog shit on the bottom of her shoe.

She had flipped me off, in fact.

And today, the rumor mill in this dinky high school was pouring out the gossip that she and I were an item.

"Are you and Briar like...a couple?" Kristy Lidel asked me where I was enjoying my lunch in the quad.

I had heard the rumblings before she asked, but she was the first to ask directly. The pack of people I hung out with waited for my answer. I could sense their ears pricking up, all of them wondering, but Kristy was the only one brave enough to ask.

"Seems like that would be between Briar and me." I took a bite of the extra chicken wrap my mom had made for Crispin and me.

I looked up to meet Crispin's expression. He rolled his eyes, knowing full well that Briar and I weren't dating. We weren't allowed to date. If my mom and dad even got a whiff of us hanging around a girl at school for too long, my dad would sit down and have *the talk* with us.

The "*Do you want to drink a young girl's veins dry accidentally*" talk.

My parents were overprotective. My mom still asked if I wanted her to go with me to the dentist. My dad was overly conscious of every extracurricular and every party or non-school event we attended.

But what other options were there for parents of young blood-sucking high school monsters? One must be vigilant.

"I didn't know you were into that kind of girl," Kristy huffed as I chewed the last bite of my wrap and pulled out a protein bar I had stashed in my backpack.

"What sort of girl?" I asked, knowing full well what she meant but hoping the shame of her thoughts would make her rethink her choice of words.

This was Kristy, however, and that was wishful thinking.

"You know she's... bigger...and kinda tall...it's totally not feminine at all."

"That's the stupidest thing I've ever heard," Crispin answered, saying what I was thinking. Not that I would have ever worded it like that.

"Your opinion is that tall women that carry more weight than you aren't feminine?" I asked with more kindness in my voice than had been in my brother's.

"Well, no, I'm not setting myself as the standard." She petulantly crossed her arms over her chest. "She's just... I mean, have you seen how she dresses, always black with her ripped tights and always in the boots? What is with the boots?"

"Jealousy is unbecoming," Crispin observed, and I shot him a disapproving look.

It was no secret that Kristy had wanted to date me almost since I walked into Ironside High and even asked me out three times. I had always come up with some excuse. Kristy was hot, without a doubt. Petite with shiny brown hair and an upturned nose, she was also popular. Kristy was cheer squad with a rich dad *popular*.

She said nothing to Crispin's blunt observation and only glared at him.

"I thought you weren't interested in dating," Kristy went on, and I cringed inwardly. She was making everyone uncomfortable now. While they all wanted to listen to my answer earlier, I bet they wished the study bell would ring now.

"Well, I'm not very interested in dating, but I am very interested in Briar." That was not a lie. I was as interested as I could be, having never interacted with her directly, aside from yesterday.

I could tell the truth and still not throw Briar under the bus. My mother always taught me never to betray a lady's confidence. I wasn't sure I was in Briar's confidence, but I didn't want to unweave whatever web she may have woven for whatever unknown reason she might have done it.

Briar was fascinating. I had thought so from the first class I took with her. I was in all her advanced courses with her, where she mostly doodled in her composition notebook the whole time. She had type 1 diabetes and wore an insulin pump, not that that made her more interesting... Well, I was a little fascinated by it. She was so dark and moody with her Bordeaux box-colored hair. She had such a bad attitude; in class, she was a ticking time bomb that could explode at any moment on one of the teachers. I found it all wildly entertaining. Her pretty dark eyes and the way her legs looked in fishnets and shorts didn't hurt either, but...she was a mystery to me. She was a walking puzzle wrapped in black band t-shirts and winged liner. I loved an exciting puzzle.

"Heads up, Loverboy," Crispin said, snatching the uneaten bar out of my hand as he passed me. "Your girl's comin'."

When I looked up, I smiled at the grumpy girl in question. I had seen her earlier in the hallway, and I nearly died of shock when she waved back at me instead of flipping me off.

"Let's give them the room," Crispin said, and I heard murmured agreement from everyone as they all began to shuffle away. Kristy moved more slowly and when Briar arrived right in front of me, she turned to look at Kristy, who was giving her the coldest glare I had seen the petite cheerleader give.

"We got a problem, Brunette Barbie?" Briar asked, and I nearly laughed out loud.

"See you at practice, Darcy," Kristy muttered before running after the others.

Once she left, Briar turned to face me. She didn't say anything at first, only took a deep breath. No doubt here to explain this strange situation to me. Or apologize, maybe?

"Hey, so I hear we are going steady." I said, rubbing the back of my neck, hoping to break some of the tension.

"Listen...Darcy."

"I'm surprised you know my name," I interrupted her, though by accident.

"Everyone knows Darcy and Crispin Booker," she quipped back, and I could tell I had already irritated her, making me smile again.

"Even the likes of Briar Grey?"

"Are you done?" Her eyes narrowed at me.

"Look at us, we just started dating, and now we are bickering like an old married couple." She didn't laugh, but I did. "Sorry, yes, I'm done. What can I do for you?"

"The thing is, I told people we're dating."

"I've heard."

"Well, I told one person, but people in this high school are like vultures for gossip."

"To be fair, it's an excellent piece of gossip. I mean…" I gestured between us; one mild-mannered, long-limbed basketball player and the school's smart-mouthed mutineer.

Her mouth quirked up in a half smile as she laughed at the contrast, and my heart did a weird stop and start in my chest.

"The thing is, I need you to pretend we are dating, which is like a big ask. I understand, but I really don't want to look like the world's biggest reject."

"It doesn't seem like you care what people think about you," I said, raising an eyebrow at her.

"Are you trying to be difficult?" She sounded exasperated.

"No," I said, leaning back against the stone wall I was standing by. "I'm just curious. I'll help you; I think you know that, but I'm curious as to why you would care about this."

"You know that I dated Morgan?" she asks, and I nod because Morgan Pope left a horrible taste in my mouth and a sinking feeling in my stomach.

"I wasn't here, but I know you did."

"And that he dumped me?"

"Yep," I said, nodding, not wanting to say that part out loud.

"And you know why he dumped me."

"I know why everyone said he dumped you. I also know that high school boys are stupid and will say untrue things to protect their fragile egos. This is coming from one such sensitive high school boy."

"Morgan is the person I told that we were dating."

"Ah." I nodded as it all came together. "You are using me to make Pope jealous? I'm slightly offended that I wasn't worth lying about for my merit alone."

That elicited another small smile.

"Not jealous, exactly. I would never get back with him after what he said and how he acted, but...."

"I get it, Briar."

"You do?"

No, I didn't get it. Morgan Pope was a tool. I could understand the female appeal, but he was still an A-class jerk. But what I could understand was that Briar needed my help, and standing there looking at me, slightly unsure, I knew I would help her. Plus, she was interesting.

Also, a fake girlfriend might help me out too. Keep Kristy off my back or anyone else who felt they needed to ask me out—having a fake relationship with someone who wouldn't expect anything beyond some light PDA to make the relationship believable might get me to the end of high school. It would make my life easier.

"I'll do this, but I need something from you."

"You need me to do your homework, Booker?" she asked.

"I'm pretty sure I get better grades than you." The words tumbled out of me, and I put my hand over my mouth in horror.

But she wasn't offended. She was smiling. What an exciting challenge she was.

"Alright, what do you need?"

"We fake date until the end of the school year."

"That's like four months!" She sounded horrified as the study bell rang, and I shouldered my backpack.

"Yeah, then we can break up for college reasons or something at graduation." I started walking away from her backward, watching panic fill her face.

"Wait, Darcy, for fuck's sake, stop! No, I didn't agree to that."

"Can you meet me in the gym after classes? If we are dating, I think you'd come to my practices, right?"

"No, no!"

"Yeah, you know what, Briar, this is a great idea." I spun around as a string of vulgar curses were yelled after me.

When I got to the door, my brother stood there waiting, expecting to be updated.

"So?" Crispin asked.

"Well, I am no longer on the singles market." I shrugged, but apparent happy energy was coming out of me. What it was from, I wasn't sure. Partly for fixing my Kristy problem, and I think part of it was working Briar up so thoroughly.

"Mom and Dad are going to slay you. Wooden steak to the heart slay, Darcy. You'll be dead before the week is out."

Chapter Four

Briar

I sat in the front seat of my car for half an hour even though the sun turned my car into an oven. Not like an oven on broil because it was January. Ironside was situated in a relatively desert area where it wasn't really cold, even in winter.

So, I was sitting in a Honda oven set to preheat not too long ago.

Basketball practice would have started already, and I was sulking. Telling myself I could drive home and completely blow off Darcy and his stupid, handsome, dorky face. I opened the car door.

I needed this. He needed to go along with it, and he had pushed back with his own terms. He had bullied me with a broad smile and a wave; I think that was what I was most upset about. I didn't like to do things I didn't want to, and Darcy Booker had me trudging to the gymnasium to pretend I was the sort of girlfriend that would watch his stupid basketball practice.

I stomped through the half-dead grass, muttering under my breath. It made me feel a little better. Being in a bad mood when doing things made me feel better somehow. While I swung the gym doors open and made my way to the bleachers of the basketball court in use, I was still defiant.

I saw the back of Darcy's head in a huddle with Mr. Dulle leading the pack. He was a tall man with serial killer blue eyes and a waxed bald head. The coach always struck me as a bit off, even though everyone else seemed to like him. He was the coach for every high school sport Ironside offered except football. Mrs. Kitch was our champion football coach. I didn't frequent football games, but she was a short and intense woman I wouldn't want to piss off.

I sat on the very edge of the bleachers. If I were lucky, no one would notice I was even here, not even Darcy.

"Briar!" a girl's voice came to me, and I turned my head to see Maisie and Trudy sitting low in the middle of the court bleachers.

I groaned quietly and smiled and nodded as they waved to me. I tried to act like I didn't know they were trying to wave me over and instead opened the laptop I had brought to do homework on.

Unfortunately, I could see out of the corner of my eye that they were gathering up their things and walking toward me.

"Jocks, I don't want to hang out with jocks," I muttered as they walked closer and closer until they were right in front of me.

Trudy was tall, taller than me, and looked like she had been born to be an athlete; the tone of her arm muscles put many of the senior boys to shame. She had dark brown skin and black hair that was always perfectly pulled back into multiple braids that she usually wore in two high buns on either side of her head. Trudy was Ironside's volleyball star. Her companion, Maisie was as short as Trudy was tall; I would be surprised if she measured taller than five foot two. She was fair with a chin-length curly bob of dark brown, but her eyes were darker still. Maisie wore a lot of pink and purple, and people called her 'princess' around the school. But when she got on the soccer field, they called her 'bulldozer,' and that contrast in personality I had always found humorous.

Maisie Pope was Morgan Pope's cousin. However, they didn't seem to run in the same circles or even talk to each other much. Whenever Morgan talked about Maisie and her family, his tone always held a bit of judgment, like he thought he was better than her.

"Hey!" Trudy said, and I looked up at them, putting on a forced smile.

"Hello." I gave a little half-wave, and any hope I had of them leaving me vanished as they dropped their stuff next to me.

"We are so excited to have another girl in the group," Trudy beamed, "We are a little outnumbered right now."

"Oh, great, maybe we can have a sleepover and paint each other's nails." I pursed my lips into a line and stared at the tall volleyball goddess whose eyes went wide, and she smiled a little bit like someone who had no idea what else to do.

"You're a bitch, just like they say, huh?" Maisie asked as Trudy covered up a laugh with a cough and came to sit beside me. She did not take my quip about the sleepover as a warning not to get close to me. I liked that in a person.

"I didn't ask you to come over here." I challenged the shorter of the girls who had a hand on her hip where she was sporting a pink pleated plaid skirt.

"We are being nice to you for Darcy. Don't flatter yourself by thinking we are here for you."

I snorted and moved my boot-clad feet so she could sit one seat down from us.

"Hey! Briar!" Darcy's voice came across the court, and I looked up as half the players turned to look at me. Their faces were a range of emotions. I caught Crispin's gaze as I scanned them, and he narrowed his eyes at me.

Darcy jogged over. He was wearing a white t-shirt, grey basketball shorts, and shoes and was already sweating into the shirt's collar. He was bouncing with energy as he stopped in front of us. He literally hopped up on the balls of his feet, alternating as he gave me one of his signature smiles.

"You being nice, Maisie?" he asked, and the small bulldozer didn't answer, but Darcy chuckled at whatever face she gave him.

"Thanks for coming," he addressed me.

"Sure," I said, unable to think of anything else.

"I'll walk you to your car after practice?"

"Why?" I frowned, but nothing I said penetrated that wide smile of straight white teeth.

"So you don't have to walk by yourself."

"I think I can handle walking to my car alone. I've been doing it for a while now."

"I'll see you after practice."

Silent bullying was turning into my least favorite thing about Darcy Booker. He winked at me and turned, jogging back to the court as the boys took their places and the practice game began.

"Licorice?" Trudy held a bag of apple-green licorice in front of me.

"I..." I started, looking at the bag as she shook it slightly, making the plastic crinkle. "...sure."

I grabbed several pieces and turned to pull my pump off, giving myself a guestimate amount of insulin before clipping it back on.

Trudy watched the game with interest, a green piece of licorice hanging from her mouth as her eyes moved with the players. Erik, her boyfriend, was in the middle of them, easily identifiable by the long curly red hair tied up on his head.

"The Booker boys don't date," Maisie said, and my eyes found hers from where she was turned to look at me with an eyebrow raised.

I closed my laptop and set my licorice on it, tearing a bite off.

"Do you have a question?" I asked, looking past her to the game I was pretending to watch. *Shit, I hated sports.*

"I didn't ask one," Maisie said, turning back around, and I let a small smile slip over my face.

I liked her.

"Thanks for the licorice," I said to Trudy, hoping that my twisted way of apologizing would come across, and if it didn't, at least I wasn't a complete bitch to her the whole time.

"What's your favorite? I'll pick some up for next practice."

"Oh, you don't have to."

Now I felt like a jerk. There was nothing worse than being rude to someone and then they were nice to you after.

"If you're hanging out with us, you're part of the group. I bring the snacks."

Pretend dating Darcy came with a whole damn teenage cult.

"I like Red Hots," I said, sighing and looking at the court again. I wouldn't mention vanilla tootsie rolls. Better to save those for the school's counselor's office. "Could someone explain basketball to me?"

I learned the basics of basketball while eating apple licorice with two girls to whom I never thought I would speak more than ten words. All this while I stared at my sweaty, basketball-playing boyfriend participating in said game. Every time he took a break, he waved to me, and I tried to avoid Crispin's glares.

Trudy and Maisie didn't talk much. They shared a few laughs at jokes I didn't understand, and Trudy let me finish her licorice. When the game was over, she got up, promising to bring me Red Hots the next day, and went to kiss Erik on his cheek as he beamed like the winner of a television show. I hadn't realized before, but Trudy was a few inches taller than Erik was.

"See you tomorrow," Maisie said, nodding to me. It wasn't a question; she knew it was slightly insulting. I chuckled a bit and saw the barest hint of a smile cross her face.

I sat on the bleachers watching Darcy say goodbye to everyone, and he walked over to me. He had this way of making me feel awkward that I didn't like.

"Thanks for sticking around. You don't have to come tomorrow if you don't want."

"Trudy is bringing me Red Hots," I said, by way of explanation for the reason I would be here in the same spot tomorrow.

It wasn't because I enjoyed the company instead of binging tv for three hours at home. It wasn't that at all.

"Red hots?" He tapped his temple with his finger. "I'll remember that as a good boyfriend would. I'm a Milk Duds guy, but I respect a woman who enjoys the classics."

"Are you going to walk me to my car now? For safety?" I got up, putting my laptop under my arm.

"I was hoping to walk with you for *my* safety. I mean, look at me; I'm prime kidnapper bait. You look like a character from Kill Bill. I feel safer with you."

"What a gentleman."

"It's the age of equality; I want to be swept off my feet. I want to be the dude in distress."

"Well, let's be off so I can protect you from the dangers of the parking lot." I started with him following closely behind me. I could feel him getting ready to talk, like the silence was offensive to him.

"Did you enjoy the practice?"

"No."

"Ah well, that's to be expected. What do you like to watch? Roller derby?"

I didn't respond to the question. Mostly because I had done roller derby when I was fourteen for a year, and despite my mother's disapproval, she still let me do it.

We ended up at my car, and I opened the door to get in, throwing my laptop into the passenger seat.

When I looked past Darcy, I saw Crispin leaning against the white truck they drove into school together. He wasn't glaring at me anymore but just looked annoyed now.

"Does your brother hate me?' I asked, tilting my head, not bothering to look away from the blond brother.

Darcy turned and looked at Cripin. "Would you wipe that look off your face? You are going to scare her off." He yelled.

"Mom texted we need to get home for dinner; wrap it up, lover boy."

"He's just grouchy that I have a new girlfriend, and he's going to live alone." He said the last bit loudly, and I heard Crispin laugh.

"Does he know that...," I inquired, not knowing what to say.

"Yeah, but he won't tell anyone else. I can't tell the others because they all have big mouths, but Crispin won't say anything."

"Won't tell anyone I'm pretending to date a jock," I said despondently. "What has my senior year come to?"

"Who knows." He knocked on the window of my open car door, and turned to walk away. "I think it could be very interesting."

Chapter Five

Darcy

"How was practice, boys?" Mom asked as she piled salad onto my plate.

"Nothing wild to report," Crispin said. "Darcy does have some news from school, though."

My eyes lifted to Crispin's slowly, and I shook my head once. I couldn't believe he was going to rat me out. But there would be no stopping the mischievous smile that crossed his face.

I ran my hands through my hair, damp from the shower I had taken before dinner.

"Oh?" My father asked, setting his phone down on the table.

The table was a phone-free zone, but it didn't apply to my dad scrolling the internet for good deals on secondhand items he didn't need—one of his favorite past times.

"What's the news, Darcy?" My mom asked, sitting next to Dad as I continued to stare at Crispin.

"Nothing; I don't have any news."

"No?" Crispin faked a confused expression rubbing his fingers over his chin. "Something about a new girlfriend is the school gossip."

"Could you fucking not?" I asked him.

"Darcy Kenton Booker," Mom warned. "No language at the table."

"Sorry," I mumbled, avoiding my dad's gaze, which was now boring into the side of my face.

"You have sixty seconds to explain your situation before I rip into you," my dad said, voice steely calm making my mind scramble for the least number of words possible to ease his concerns.

"Her name is Briar, and she isn't my girlfriend." I tried to keep the information clipped and informational. "We are just friends. She asked if I would pretend to date her until the schoolyear's end."

Sort of a lie as I was the one who insisted on the end of the school year, but there was some truth that should be shared and some truth that would get me in large amounts of trouble.

"Pretend to date her?" My dad's anger had not been sated, but he was asking questions. That was a good sign. I looked to my mom, who nodded a little for me to go on.

"She dated Morgan Pope for two years, and he kinda broke her heart; he and his friends are being dicks...."

"Darcy..." Mom reminded me.

"He and his friends are being jerks to her. They paint nasty things on her locker every day. Anyway, she asked if I would pretend to be dating her to... I don't know, make him sorry or take the spotlight off her."

I looked at my mom and saw the spark of sympathy in her eyes. I had won her over with Briar's sad story. Truth be told, winning Mom over was three-quarters of the battle. My father loved my mom more than anything in life.

"That sounds ridiculous," my dad said, looking over at my mom. His voice had softened, and I knew he needed only a bit of push to be...maybe not okay with this but avoiding *THE* lecture.

"Briar's not even Darcy's type, Dad; she's all moody, angsty, and grumpy. There is no chance she'd be interested. Have you seen Morgan Pope? He and Darcy aren't even in the same universe regarding tastes. And she has really been going through it at school." Crispin swooped in, and I fought the urge to send him a thank-you glance.

He had gotten me into this mess. The least he could do now was help me.

"I don't like you guys hanging out with the Pope kids." Dad shifted subjects, and I breathed out a little. "First Maisie, and now what is this about Morgan...."

"They don't know what we are, Dad," Crispin assured him.

What we were.

Too many names for it to count, vampires being the most prolific. *Bloodsuckers. Leeches. Devourers. Nightwalkers. Demons. gods.*

"Plus, I don't think Maisie is like that," I said.

"Darcy, you never know with hunters. Some of them are reformed to new ways, but many still clung to old traditions. Your friend might be nice, but if she ever found out what you were, she could turn on you just as easily. Same with Morgan Pope. The Popes are the only hunter family in a hundred-mile radius, that's why we picked this town, but you still have to be careful."

"Nolan," my mother's voice was soft and correcting as my father took a long breath and ran his hands over his face.

Crispin and I had gone silent as the cloud of reality hung over the dinner table. The truth of what we were and how it made our lives different. Always moving, always hiding, always getting lectures from Dad, who was just worried. Every day we went to public school, he received another grey hair at his temples.

"I'm sorry, boys." He exhaled, taking his hands from his face. "I trust you both. I know you are smart boys, young men. You have grown up, and I know you know the rules. You've never given us pushback on them. I don't mean to come down on you."

"We know," Crispin answers, nodding and taking a bite of salad.

"So, Briar," Mom says, changing the subject. "Will you bring her for dinner?"

"She's just my fake girlfriend, Mom. She doesn't need to come for dinner."

"I can make fake dinner." She laughed at her joke, but no one else did as the table grew silent.

I reached for my cup of blood and drained the thick cold liquid wiping some off my mouth with the back of my hand. Vampires have to eat food like the rest of the human race. We just also have to drink blood. A bit every day, or we get hungry and desperate. Then we get sick and eventually die if we don't have any. It would take a good three weeks for you to die, but a famished vampire is not the sort you want to run into.

Teenage vampires are worse. We needed twice the amount of blood child or adult vampires might. Our urges are more assertive, and we have less control over everything. That's why my dad worries so much—the reason most vampires are homeschooled. The risks are high. But my parents keep us well-fed, and we have strict parameters to ensure an accident doesn't happen.

1. No dating.

2. No skipping blood meals.

3. Continuously being enrolled in a physical sport. (The physical strain helps with the urges)

A litany of other small rules, but those are the main ones. The blood we drank was from blood bags. The Guild made sure to donate plenty to certain hospitals across the world. So you could look up which would supply you in your area. The hospital here in Ironside was forty-five miles away, but we had driven further.

I picked my cup back up and stuck two fingers inside, collecting the blood that coated the side. I watched it drip off my fingers back into the cup as I thought of what it would be like to live an ordinary high school life.

"Darcy," my mom warned again.

I figured I should finish dinner without incident since that was the third time she had said my name like that. I put my cup down and licked my fingers clean smiling an apology. I polished off all the food on my plate, offering no less than three compliments on my mother's cooking, which she accepted with a roll of her eyes.

Crispin and I cleared the table and did the dishes before shuffling up to our rooms to do homework before bed.

"Sorry," Crispin said as we headed up the stairs. "I didn't mean for it to get so...."

"It's fine. I was going to tell them anyway," I said, shrugging.

And that was that. Crispin was my older brother, and older brothers are annoying as shit, but there was no one on this planet I felt more loyal to. Plus, he was only six months older than me. My parents had adopted him as a baby when their friends had been killed. They had been his legal godparents and guardians, just as Crispin's biological parents had been mine.

The accident was as specific as Mom and Dad would get, but both Crispin and I suspected hunters killed them, which is why our parents were so overbearing now. When you lost people you loved, you tried to protect everyone else from that.

I sat at the computer for about an hour, scribbling through my math homework before shutting my laptop and going to flop myself on my bed.

My thoughts turned to Eriar and the glimpses I saw of her during practice. She was so absorbing. Not like any girl I had met before. She wanted so badly to be irritated about everything. I could see her trying to be irritated. I had never met someone who tried so hard to be...contrary.

It made her infrequent smiles and small fits of laughter addicting. Who was I to make such a girl laugh? Oh, but I wanted to be the guy that made the girl who hated everything laugh.

I didn't need to be her real boyfriend. I wasn't even sure I wanted to be. I didn't need to touch her. I didn't need to kiss her. I could live with not seeing what she looked like naked. Abiding by my parents' rules kept people safe, safe from me.

If only I could get her to smile or laugh once a day. Or at least every day I saw her.

Yeah. This would be fun.

Chapter Six

Briar

I waited at the entrance to the school for Darcy. Mostly because I had seen Morgan walk in before me, and he caught my eye looking back. I knew the signs when he wanted to talk to me, and I was not in the mood. I was never in the mood, but especially not today.

I had woken up in my own blood after starting my period four days early. I had dumped my coffee on the floor and hit every red light on the way to school. Also, there was not a single good song that came on my shuffled playlist, no matter how much skipping I did. It wasn't my day; I could feel it all the way to my big left toe that was sticking out of a hole in my black knee-high socks.

"You waited for me," Darcy said, and I looked up to see him and Crispin approaching.

Darcy and Crispin were the closest brothers I knew. Standing next to each other, they didn't look related at all. Where Darcy had soft features and bright blue eyes, Crispin had sharper, harder bone structure, blond hair, and dark eyes. Not to mention that Darcy dressed almost exclusively in athletic wear with messy hair like he just rolled out of bed every day. Crispin always looked comfortable but very put together. He had diamond studs in each of his ears, and I had noticed his nails painted a pearlescent translucent white the day before.

Darcy walked with kindness. He seemed more approachable despite being at least a few inches taller than Crispin. Crispin didn't seem unfriendly... maybe a bit more 'fuck around and find out.'

"It's downright sweet that you've melted the heart of the school's scene girl," Crispin said as he passed us and went to walk into the school, leaving Darcy and me alone outside.

He walked by too fast for me to flip him off, and I narrowed my eye at the closing door.

"Can I carry your backpack?" He held his hand out to me, and I stared up at him, unmoving.

"What is this, the nineteen-sixties?" I tightened the grip on the straps that I was holding.

"I didn't say anything about sticking my hand in your back pocket or asking what you plan on making me for dinner. I just offered to carry your book bag."

"I can carry it myself."

"Briar," he said, slightly condescending, but there was too much honey in it to stir up anger. "Give me the bag."

We stared at each other. He kept his hand out and smiled. I rolled my eyes, took my black and white checkered backpack off my shoulders, and handed it to him. I walked over to the doors.

"Well, you better open them for me. If I try, I may faint."

"Don't mind if I do." He smiled and opened the door, unaffected by my salty attitude. At least one of us was in a good mood today. However, Darcy Booker may have been in a good mood every day.

"You drop your books off in your locker first?" he asked as we walked down the halls that were very nearly empty as the bell rang a minute ago.

"Normally, but I don't have time today. I'll take it to class and put it in there at my next class change."

"Sorry, we are always late; Crispin had to primp before we came. I always wait in the car for him for twenty minutes at least."

I went to say no problem but then decided to be silent instead. I could already feel his good mood affecting me, lifting my spirits. I didn't want that. I wanted to be mad about my spilled coffee.

"I spilled my coffee in my car today," I shared, trying to recall the incident and the anger that came along with it. "And I started my damn period early. Fucking blood all over my sheets."

I side-eyed him. You could tell a lot about a guy by how he acted when you brought your period up.

"Oh, geez, I'm sorry about that. Sounds like a drag." He sounded genuine and didn't make any faces like he was grossed out. "And then the coffee, no wonder you had a grumpy face when I walked up."

"That's just my face." I cracked a half smile.

"It was extra grumpy today. You have bitch resting face for sure, but this morning it seemed like maybe I had already done something to piss you off. I'm glad it's just your bodily function and loss of the drink, and I am not to blame."

We stopped in front of the door to my first class, and I held out my hand to receive my backpack. I was aware that all eyes in the classroom were on us as he handed it to me with a smile.

"Same time tomorrow?"

"Not if you show up late. I'll have to carry my own stuff in."

"Oh, I can't have that, I'll tell Crispin he needs to be on time, or he's on his own. The beautiful Briar Grey can't be carrying her bookbag. Not while I'm around." He booped my nose with the tip of one of his pointer fingers.

I was warm and not in a nice way but in the 'I am going to explode with awkward energy' sort of way. He was a much better actor than I was an actress. I couldn't even respond as he walked away, my cheeks feeling sunburned.

I turned to walk into my classroom, and the teacher, Mrs. Holland, openly stared at me. She didn't even say anything about me being tardy. She just stared like the rest of the class at the awkward pairing that Darcy and I had made.

"Sorry, Mrs. Holland," I mumbled on the way to my seat.

Looking back at her, she seemed taken aback that I had even apologized.

Mrs. Holland was one of the good teachers at Ironside. By good, I mean she left me alone, and I left her alone. She had never once given me detention, and I didn't mouth off to her. I don't even think she was thirty yet. She looked young and pretty. She dressed a little more trendy than the other teachers and gave off that 'you can talk to me' vibe. She was short, really short, and never wore heels. She often struggled to reach things.

Despite that, none of the other students messed with Mrs. Holland either. For one, she had moved to town and married the fire chief's son, Jeremiah, a hotshot firefighter. All the boys in school treated him like he was a war hero or something. And second, once a junior had written an erotic love letter to her on the top of the board where she couldn't reach. When she had gotten a stool and dragged it to the whiteboard, the class had snickered until she tore the entire thing apart grammatically. She made fun of it so much that I doubted whoever did it would ever come forward.

I checked my pump as she began to go over homework, rolling my eyes at the high number despite having carb-counted my breakfast. I gave myself some corrections and looked forward.

I would have to put in an order for pump supplies soon, which meant telling my mom I needed around six hundred dollars for the out-of-pocket cost. I let out a sigh and clipped my pump back onto my shorts.

I listened to Mrs. Holland go on about what would be on the upcoming test. I took notes on what I thought I might need to study. My embarrassment had died off, and I was hardly even thinking of Darcy touching my nose.

"Are you and Booker really dating?" a girl name Meera leaned over and asked me. I sat next to Meera in this class every other day. She was a cheerleader with golden skin and thick dark hair that she wore in curly waves around her face.

"No," I rolled my eyes at her. "We are fake dating."

She chuckled at the truth that I had intentionally used to lie.

"Cool, he's nice. I didn't think he dated," she whispered because Mrs. Holland shot us a glare.

I didn't think that the side effect of dating Darcy might be that people who had ignored me might try to talk to me now. Meera had never once tried to speak to me since the beginning of the year.

Was being seen with him making me approachable? Oh, I was not too fond of the thought of that.

Chapter Seven

Darcy

We were walking back from the gas station across the street from the school when Morgan flagged me down. He was smoking by the fence line with some of his buddies, and I groaned inwardly. Whatever conversation I was about to have, I didn't want to have it.

"You want me to come with you?" Crispin asked.

"No, but if he starts to kick my ass, just promise not to film it."

"I might film a little bit, but then I'll come help."

"Thanks so much." I handed him the iced coffee I had gotten for Briar and jogged over to Morgan, to whom I don't think I had ever spoken more than ten words.

"Will you give us a minute," Morgan said to the two guys and the girl he had been going with for a couple of months. I couldn't remember her name.

They all walked off, leaving us standing awkwardly together.

"What's sup, buddy?" I inquired, sticking my hands in the pockets of my basketball shorts.

"I wanted to talk about this thing with you dating Briar."

My stomach dropped as I frowned. It wasn't like I was surprised. What other reason could he have for talking to me? I had been hoping it wouldn't come up. But with guys like Morgan Pope, that was never the case. The guy walked around our school like a peacock with his feathers displayed.

He took a drag from his cigarette and then dropped it onto the sidewalk below, stepping on it with the tip of his boot. Maisie smoked, too. It must have been a family thing.

"Okay," I responded, resisting the urge to shuffle my feet.

"I think you should leave her alone."

I let the words sit there for a minute, not needing to respond quickly.

"Why is that?"

"You know why."

My heartbeat picked up because I did know why, but did he know why?

"I don't think I do." I kept my voice even and slightly confused.

"People like us aren't good for anyone."

"People like us?" Now I was confused. "No offense Pope, but you and I have little to no similarities."

"I think we are more alike than you might think." He said it while looking directly into my eyes, and I hoped my face didn't appear like I thought he was the world's foremost crazy person.

"It's bad enough that Maisie has decided to hang out with you and your brother, but at least she is making an informed choice."

The conversation was going somewhere that would create too much of a problem for me. Anxiety welled up in me, and I felt my heart beat slow. I could hear Morgan's heartbeat increase as my heightened senses kicked in. Whenever my heart rate increased, or I felt any heightened emotion, my senses went into overdrive. I could hear everything, smell everything.

I needed to extract myself from this situation before my anxiety increased. Before my fangs came out.

"Okay buddy, well, this was a great chat...." I went to walk away, but he reached out and grabbed my arm.

"I don't think you are hearing me."

"Please get your hand off of me," I said, pulling it out of his grasp.

"I said you need to stay away from her."

"Listen, Morgan, I don't know what your damage is, dude, but if you have a problem with Briar dating me, you should bring it up with her. Because while I may not have known her for very long, I know she would kick your ass up and down the football field if you tried to tell her what to do."

Crispin walked over to me in what others might observe as casual, but I saw the tension in his jaw.

"Everything fine, Darcy?"

"Yeah, I think so. Let's get to practice." I went to walk away and turned back to look at Morgan, who was lighting another cigarette; his face red with anger.

"Another thing is, for how much you seem to be worried about Briar; you would think you could keep your friends from tagging her locker every other day. Just some food for thought. See you around."

"You need me to kick his ass?" Crispin asked when we were far enough away.

"Nah, he's just pressed he lost the girl."

"Rumor is he broke up with her."

"That might be the rumor, dude, but that's not what his body language was saying to me. He still thinks she belongs to him. Also, he pretty much insinuated he knows."

"Knows what?" Crispin asked, but the edge to his voice let me know I didn't need to answer.

I shook off the conversation. I was going to work it off in practice and forget how Morgan stared into my eyes and threatened to expose me because of a girl.

We walked into the gym, and I smiled, seeing Briar already sitting with the girls. I took her coffee from Crispin thinking I wasn't sure I could blame him for not being over Briar. When she scowled at me, something warmed inside me.

"I brought you a coffee, you know, for the one that spilled this morning but then thought maybe you don't drink coffee in the afternoon," I said, holding it out to her.

"No, I'll pretty much drink it anytime," she said, taking it and immediately taking a sip through the straw. She made a face quickly.

"Not good."

"It's just got sugar." She took another sip to make a show of still drinking it.

"Makes sense you don't drink it with sugar," I said, taking my hoodie off and setting it next to her. "You're sweet enough already."

"Go," she said, pointing to the court, her cheeks coloring pink just like they had this morning.

I didn't argue or push her further because Morgan's conversation was still playing in my head, and I needed to start moving.

"I think your plan is working," I said once we reached Briar's car after practice.

"My plan?"

"Morgan flagged me down before practice."

"He did?" she asked, and there was a touch too much hope in her voice.

I thought then that Briar might still be in love with Morgan Pope. She usually sounded so distant or uninterested. This was the most curious I had heard her be.

"He did. Told me to stay away from you."

She frowned then, and for some reason, I counted that as a point for myself.

"What did you say?"

"I told him he should talk to you about it if he had a problem. Kind of seemed like he thought he still was in charge of you."

She leaned back against her car and took a deep breath rolling her head around.

"I'd love to tell you he isn't in charge of me, but I can't commit to that statement, can I? I am doing all this to...get back at him...make him jealous? I don't know what I'm doing."

Honest. I liked that in her.

"Well, whatever you wanted, you got his attention, and subsequently, so do I."

She winced a little. "Sorry about that. He wasn't rude to you, was he?"

"Oh, he definitely was. Maybe it was just his face, though."

"No, he's just a dick." She laughed loudly, and I smiled, rubbing the back of my neck.

"Some of us are going to the roller rink tomorrow night. Would you like to go?"

"The roller rink? On a Saturday night? It's going to be slammed."

"It normally is, but they play the best music and do black lights and disco balls. Plus, everyone from school goes. Could be a good opportunity to show up as a couple."

"Would you be upset if I said no?" she asked me, and I opened my mouth to tell her, *of course not*, but then shut it. She had never been anything but honest with me, and I felt like returning the favor, so I thought about it.

"Well, Briar, I like you. I think you're interesting. If I didn't like you, I wouldn't have agreed to fake date you, so...yeah, I want you to go, but I won't be upset if you decide not to go. Doesn't have to be your thing."

"Can I think about it?"

"Give me your phone," I said, holding out my hand, and she hesitantly took her phone out of her back pocket and handed it to me. I typed my number into her phone, took a selfie with a big smile and a peace sign, and handed it back to her after texting my own number.

"Boyfriend Material?" she asked, smirking at the name I had chosen for myself.

"Text me tomorrow if you want to go. I can pick you up if you want." I waved to her as I walked away.

When I got into the truck with Crispin, a heavy silence filled the cab as he pulled out of the parking lot.

"So, do we tell Mom and Dad or not?" he asked as I closed my eyes and wished for the ten thousandth time I was not a seventeen-year-old vampire.

Chapter Eight

Briar

"You should go."

"I should not go."

"Why wouldn't you go?"

"Why would I go?"

My best friend sighed over the phone, and I could hear her patience growing thin through the airwaves.

"How sure are you that your parents won't let you out of your annual trip to Mexico to save me from this fake date?"

"Ma!" I heard Triana shout as she posed the question to her mother in Spanish. I listened to her mother, Sara, laugh happily in the background and shout back something muffled.

"Hell has a better chance at freezing over. Plus, I like this trip, so there's no way I would stay to bail you out, sorry friend."

"Wow, where is the loyalty?"

"Guess I don't love you that much."

"Maybe I'll go to Mexico with you. Disappear for a few weeks."

"You know my parents would never turn you away, but we leave in two days, my love, and you have neither a passport nor a plane ticket."

"Shove me in your luggage."

Triana laughed half-heartedly

It was true that the Mendez family would never turn me away. Sara Mendez was my second mom pretty much and had fed me more than my mom had in elementary and middle school. Though she never disparaged my mom for working a lot. She always told me my mom was strong enough to do what she had to.

She had even slightly inspired my love of cooking. Since I was always around like a stray cat on their back porch, she taught me to cook things that her mother had taught her to cook. I still went to their house every December and helped make Christmas tamales. It was a long day of laughter, teasing, and an assembly line of the best kind.

For some reason, my eyes pricked with tears thinking of how much I missed them. Once I saw them three or four times a week. Now, I saw Triana once a week and hardly saw the Mendez's at all.

"Tell your family I love them," I said, getting up from where I was lying on my bed to look at their Christmas card from last year.

Triana's school took a three-week winter break, so she would only be missing a week. Her summers were shorter, but it worked for her parent's travel habits.

"I will, and they love you back," she responded.

"Four weeks without seeing you," I whined again, feeling desperately needy. "I don't have any friends, Tri. You can't do this to me."

"So go to the damned roller rink and make some, and you better not replace me either. Do you hear me? I am not giving up my spot as best friend to anyone. So make some new friends but they better not be as cool as me."

"There's a girl named Maisie; I think you would like her. She's...not gonna put up with my shit."

"I already like her."

I heard Mrs. Mendez holler something in the background.

"I gotta go, B," Triana sighed.

"I'll talk to you in three weeks, and you can text me while I'm away. I might not respond super-fast."

"I'll keep you updated on my fake dating life."

"Speaking of, go get ready for your fake date now."

"Love you."

"Love you more."

"Love you most."

Click

It was almost two, too late to text Darcy and ask if I could go. He hadn't texted me to ask if I wanted to. He said he would, but perhaps he was tired of my blatant hesitation.

I tossed the phone on the bed and walked to my door, but my text tone went off before I could exit the room. I stared at it, leaning my head against the doorframe.

I left it on the bed and walked to the kitchen to open the fridge. I needed to go grocery shopping tomorrow. I was staring at three jars of different pickles, condiments, half a carton of eggs, and lettuce that had seen better days. I reached out and grabbed a can of tonic water and popped it open, walking back to my bed and reaching for the phone.

Boyfriend Material: Pick you up at 5?

While staring at the message, I got one from Triana.

TriTri: Let me see the date fit

I took a picture of me on my bed with terrible posture in the rainbow tie dye and some ripped oversized jeans.

TriTri: You can't be serious. Change. Do something with your hair. For goodness sake, put on some eyeliner. Look like you care.

Briar: I don't care

TriTri: Change.

"Fucking fuck." I stuck my tongue out at the phone, switching to Darcy's text.

Briar: You know where I live?

Boyfriend Material: No, I had hoped you would share your address with me. I am willing to go door to door, however. Just let me know because I'll have to leave earlier than anticipated.

Briar: 1337 Cast Court apartment 6, smartass.

Boyfriend Material: ;) see you then!

I got up, went to my drawers, and pulled out a black tee shirt that said *emotionally exhausted* in wavy rainbow letters. I searched in the pile of clothes that were 'bottoms clean enough to wear.' I pulled out a pair of distressed denim shorts and unbuttoned my pants, and sighed as I realized I would have to shower and shave if I was wearing shorts. I threw the clothes on my bed, stalking to the bathroom.

"I don't even have a real boyfriend, and I have to shave," I grumbled, turning on the hot water.

❧

I took an updated picture for Triana after swiping on some eyeliner, tinted ChapStick, and mascara. I wasn't wearing any tights, just some black and white striped knee highs with shorts and the t-shirt. I had dried my hair and thrown half of it back so it wouldn't get in my way when I was skating.

TriTri: Looking FINE, Girl.

I went into the bathroom and spritzed myself with the perfume that my mom got me for Christmas. I realized I hadn't put this much thought into an outfit since I had been dating Morgan.

As I left my room to wait in the living room my pump tubing snagged on my door handle and I felt the familiar sting of the small needle site being ripped off of me. I hollered a loud stream of curse words and stalked back into my room to replace the damn thing.

Once I was done I sat on the couch and nursed my irritation with the half can of tonic water I had let sit out. I also grabbed some schoolwork to work on until five.

Five turned out to be four forty-five, and there was a knock on my door.

I set my laptop next to me and got up. For some reason, I found my heart racing a bit, and I was nervous. I shook it off, opened the door, and was greeted by Darcy's smiling face over two bouquets.

"What are those?"

"Hello Briar, how are you this evening? Might I come in?"

I didn't answer him but stepped aside so he could come into our apartment.

"The white ones are for you; the yellow ones are for your mom," he said, handing over the flowers, and I stared at them like he was a cat that had just brought me a dead animal.

"What the fuck is wrong with you?" I asked, dragging my gaze from him to the flowers and then back to him.

He moved around me and walked surveyed the apartment, helping himself to a tour of the kitchen.

"What specifically do you mean? There are lots of things to pick from."

"Who brings flowers to a fake date? Who brings flowers to a regular date?"

"You're always so angry about the strangest things."

"I'm not mad."

"You seem mad." He leaned down a bit to view all the pictures on the fridge.

He was wearing some grey joggers and a black Adidas T-shirt. I realized his t-shirts always looked too big for him, but I supposed he had to buy them big so they would extend his long torso.

"You know how to skate?" he asked, turning around with his hands in his pockets.

"A little." I smiled knowingly, going to see if my mom had anything that could be used as a vase.

Chapter Nine

Darcy

She smelled divine. Not that her perfume was permeating off her like an old lady wearing too much musk, but I could smell things better than most humans.

The truck's cabin smelled so fantastic I was struggling not to breathe in too deeply and expose myself for the weirdo I was. It was like oranges, coconut, and something else—Something sweeter and sandalwood, maybe, with some flowers. I was picking up all the notes of whatever perfume she had put on. I wasn't usually a perfume fan. Too cloying, too liberally applied, walking through high school might as well have been one giant Bath and Body Works mixed with the axe section from the local grocery store.

"You smell nice," I said, pulling out of her driveway, my hand on the back of the seat as I turned to look behind me.

She didn't respond. She did that a lot when I said things; simply did not reply. I wondered if it was because she couldn't think of something rude enough to say or maybe she couldn't think of anything nice. I was still figuring it out.

"I'm a little nervous that you have your own skates; it's kind of like when you invite someone bowling, and they bring their own bowling ball."

"You been bowling a lot lately?" She asked, giving me a side eye from the passenger seat. "On the local silver senior team, are you, Booker?"

"I take sports very seriously, plus it's a great place to pick up on ladies. A little grey never bothered me."

She laughed outright. I preened inside like I had just beat Ripley's world record.

"Gross." She got out around her laughter. "First, I hear you don't date, and now you're chasing old ladies in assisted living homes."

"I'm a mysterious man." I shrugged. "What can I say?"

"Maisie told me you and Crispin don't date."

"Did she? Well, she's right; we don't."

"Why?"

"Personal choice. High school relationships are messy and rarely produce anything of substance. So, it just seems better to focus on grades and sports until we mature."

That is the story we stuck to. The lines we fed people because it was weirder to say our parents wouldn't let us, especially when Crispin was eighteen and I was a few weeks away from my eighteenth birthday.

"I don't know what I expected, but it wasn't that." She sat back in her seat, making herself comfortable, and looked out her window.

"Where's Crispin?"

"Erik and Trudy picked him up. He'll be at the rink."

"Why didn't he ride with you?" she asked, confused.

"Briar, have you forgotten already that we are fake dating?"

"No…" Her head turned to mine, a fire in her eyes like she was ready to go toe to toe with me verbally.

"Well, how romantic would it be if I picked up my girlfriend for our first date with my brother in the car?"

She didn't respond but turned and looked back out the window.

When we reached the roller rink, the parking lot was nearly full. Briar had been right; it was slammed. The thing about small towns is that all the teenagers gathered in the same areas.

I got out of the truck and opened Briar's door. I thought she might not let me, but she was too busy looking at the sea of cars and the people streaming in and out of the entrance. When I opened the door, she looked a little pale, and as I focused on her, I could tell her heart rate had increased.

"You, okay?" I asked, leaning into the car.

"Yeah, I just...." She trailed off. "I don't love large crowds, and I do it at school but not normally by choice... like at the mall, I hate the mall, I order clothes online because I hate it so much."

"Got it." I nodded.

Crispin had always been a little more to himself. I think he forced himself to go out a lot for my sake. I liked to be around people. I looked forward to large gatherings and didn't feel as drained as my brother. So I couldn't understand exactly what she was saying, but I understood its validity.

"Do you want to go home? Do something else? We can go see a movie or something?"

"No, everyone will be here; you're right. You're pulling your weight in the fake relationship, and I can pull mine." Her face looked a little hesitant. "I'm sorry I was a dick about the flowers. They were nice. I'm grateful you agreed to do this. I'm sorry I'm a dick."

"You are kinda a dick," I agreed, hoping to alleviate some of the anxiety she was feeling.

She chuckled, and I stepped back as she climbed out of the truck.

"Can I hold your hand?" I asked as we walked through the parking lot.

"No, but you can hold my skates." She held out her skates, and I took them.

"Seeing how I have to fight you on holding the backpack, I'll take it."

We walked in side by side, with me holding her skates and her looking a little less queasy than she had looked in the car. When we entered the door, I scanned the crowded place for my friends and caught Crispin's waving hand on the other side of the check-in counter.

We registered with mild panic from the woman working when I asked for a size fourteen shoe, and mild complaining from Briar when I paid for us both. Other than those two things not too dramatic. When we ended up at the table where the crew was, I saw they had all changed into their skates and were waiting on us.

"Your first date, Briar, was Darcy a gentleman?" Trudy asked, sitting on a bench next to Erik, who wagged his eyebrow at me.

"He opened all the doors for me and brought me and my mom flowers."

Maisie snorted, and Trudy smacked Erik on the arm lightly.

"What's that for?" Erik asked.

"Opening doors? Flowers for a date? Do you hear that? Where are my flowers?"

"They just started dating. Wait until the puppy love goes away." Erik rolled his eyes and leaned in to kiss Trudy, but she pulled back.

"Are you saying you aren't in puppy love with me?"

"I feel like this is a trap." My friend ran his hand through his red hair and squinted at me. "This is your fault."

"Better step up your game, man. Just because you have the girl now doesn't mean she won't realize there are more freckled red-heads in the sea."

"Exactly," Trudy agreed. "Thank you, Darcy gets it."

"My love, my life, I will open every door and buy you every flower." Erik crooned and went in for another kiss which she accepted, and we all looked away like we always did.

"You ready?" I heard Briar ask from where she had already laced up her skates.

"You coming out, Crispin? Not worried about breaking a nail?" Maisie asked, skating to the opening in the rink as I sat down to put my skates on.

"Go on, Princess; I'll give you a head start." Crispin fired back, standing up to follow her out.

I got my skates on, set my tennis shoes with the rest of our stuff, and skated over to Briar, who was waiting for me at the entrance.

"We going in?" she asked.

"Oh, I stay on the outside, but you go ahead. I just hug the wall."

"You what?" she asked, horrified.

"I think it's like my height and the long legs. You know I'm not built for the skating rink, no matter how much I practice. Crispin says I look like a baby giraffe."

I clambered into the entrance and held into the outside wall like a child learning to walk as my knees nearly buckled.

"Hold on." Briar pushed passed me and started doing a lap around the rink, and I stayed still, watching her in awe as she confidently skated around people with a little more flair than necessary. She slid backward when she passed Trudy, who laughed and said something to her.

The lights went dim as a colorful strobe began to flash, throwing lights all over the walls. The song Push-It started to play as the energy in the room shifted, and my fake girlfriend did a little twirl on her way back to me.

"You skate a little?" I asked, leaning my butt against the wall and kicking my skates out.

"I had to get one good lap in before I babied you the rest of the time. Come on, skate with me."

"Oh no, you go, please. I don't belong out there in the wild; I'm fine."

"Can I hold your hand?" She held her hand out to me, and I couldn't bring myself to deny her.

I don't even think I wanted to.

Not even a little.

Chapter Ten

Briar

Darcy walked me to my apartment door despite my insistence that he didn't have to.

He had paid for everything, my entry into the skating rink, my grilled cheese from the little food counter. He even did the cheesy boyfriend thing and won me a stuffed animal from a claw machine game. I'd never actually seen someone win one, but he did, and I was now the owner of a monochromatic purple fox which he named Lucy for me. It was pretty cute. Not that I would say that out loud.

I expected it to be awkward when I went in. To do that thing you sometimes do with people when you first hang out. The strange linger on the porch while you shuffle your feet. In those moments, I usually just walked away with a curt goodbye.

But it wasn't awkward with Darcy. He walked me up to the porch and nodded for me to open the door, and once it was open, he started walking away backward.

"Admit that tonight wasn't completely horrible," he said, his voice blending with the warm air and the crickets chirping.

"I won't say that."

"Admit defeat, Grey, come on."

"Never." I went inside and closed the door behind me to the sound of his low laughter.

"Hey, baby girl."

I shrieked and turned around, gripping my stuffed animal to my chest.

My mother stared at me wide-eyed and took a step away from me.

"Holy hell, Mom," I said, relaxing.

"I'm sorry, B; I texted you to tell you I came home a little early. You on edge?"

"No, sorry, my phone died on the way home."

"Out with Tri? Where are the flowers from? Did you pick them up from the store?"

Here we were, where I could tell my mom about Darcy. I could lie and say he was just my friend, which I suppose wasn't totally a lie. If I told her he was my boyfriend, she might feel better about me moving on from Morgan. But she may worry more when Darcy and I "broke up" right after graduation. The lines of thought were endless.

"They are from Darcy. Yellow ones are for you," I supplied, letting her conclude.

"New friend?" she asked, walking me to the kitchen, where she stuck her nose into the yellow blooms.

"Boyfriend." I turned, opening the fridge. "You hungry? Want me to make you something?"

"Oh no, no, no, we aren't just going to let that slide on by without addressing it. Tell me more about this boyfriend."

I sighed, knowing she would find a way to work questions into all our following conversations if I didn't. I plugged my phone into a charger, waited for it to power up, and pulled up my Instagram. My profile was bare as the desert, but I liked seeing the pictures Triana posted. I typed in Darcy's name, and his handle, **@bookerup71,** popped on the screen. I scrolled through some of the photographs, mostly of others, not himself. My giant of a boyfriend wasn't one for selfies.

When I finally found one of him and Crispin standing next to each other in their basketball uniforms, I turned it to show my mom.

"Which one? The pretty boy?"

"No, Mom, the tall one."

"Ah, he's cute. How tall is he, goodness gracious."

"He's tall."

"Basketball player?"

"Yep," I acknowledged. "You're like Sherlock Holmes."

"You better watch your mouth, little girl, don't sass me. I brought you into this world, and I sure as shit can take you out," she said, but she chuckled as there was no real threat. "Athletic, tall, he looks friendly. Not your type, is he?"

"No," I agreed. "But he's nice. He brought me flowers for the date we just had; he opened my door. He's kinda a dork...well, he's a huge dork. A very tall dorky sweet guy."

"Oh?"

I looked at her over the fridge door, knowing she wanted to say something.

"What?"

"Nothing."

"Not nothing. You just gave me the mom *oh*."

I knew why she was hesitating. I was volatile. Even with my mother, I loved her so much, but my tongue was sharp as a razor blade, just waiting for a chance to say something contrary.

"I'll be nice," I promised.

"Pick the good boy, Briar. That is all I was going to say. Make your forever boy be the one who opens your door and brings your mom flowers."

I would have made fun of her, but her voice had cracked a little, and I got the sinking feeling that she may not have picked the good boy. I wasn't going to ask her, so I just nodded as she blinked up at the ceiling to bring her tears back.

"We've only been dating for like three days, so we don't have to talk about picking anyone yet. I don't want to do long distance when he goes to college either, and I think he's off to a faraway land." I really didn't know if that was true, but I wanted to move on from this.

"Can you bring him by the bar next weekend?" She asked it so casually that I almost smiled.

"I'll text and ask."

I followed Darcy and put my phone in my back pocket as my pump beeped at me. I unclipped it from my shorts and groaned, realizing it was out of insulin. I had gotten a warning before I ate at the roller rink. It was time to pay the piper and install a new injection site.

"How about we do popcorn and snacks and watch a movie? I'm never home this early."

"Yeah, sounds good!"

"I'll run to the corner market. What kind of snack do you want?"

I'd already had so many carbs earlier in the day. So, I thought through a litany of snacks that I wouldn't need to take a copious amount of insulin to eat.

"Pork rinds?" I asked. "Maybe a Coke Zero?"

"You've got it. Why don't you change into your pajamas and pick the movie, and I'll be right back."

I nodded and felt a knot forming in my stomach as I thought of asking her what I needed to. I shut the fridge and went to the front door to take off my shoes.

"I've got to order some pump supplies."

"Okay, Baby, how much do you need?"

I calmed the anxiety that was clawing up my throat. We had mediocre private insurance, but diabetes was still costly. It was expensive to live.

"I need to order some extras like skin film and alcohol wipes; I can order those online, though see if I can get them cheaper."

"Briar, you don't need to scour the internet for cheaper medical supplies. Just let me know how much you need, and I'll transfer it over when you are ready to order."

"Okay, Mom."

"You aren't a burden," she said, giving me a half hug and a kiss on my forehead as she went back out the front door.

I was glad the door closed on my tears so my mom didn't see them. She said the same thing every few months when I had to ask her for money to order more supplies. I tried to use my insulin and supplies wisely, so I didn't use more than needed. Even though when I said that to my mom, she would get upset with me.

Briar, you are a teenager; eat the damn pizza without worrying about how much insulin I will have to pay for it.

So, I didn't talk about it. But in my mind, I was always conscious of how much insulin I was using, trying to make it last as long as possible—not eating things, packing my low-carb snacks. A tiny sliver of guilt would always creep up when I ate something high-carb, like at the roller rink.

You aren't a burden.

I sure as shit felt like one.

Chapter Eleven

Darcy

"We'll be fine," Crispin assured me as we drove to school on Tuesday.

My parents had gone to get our regular blood order on Saturday. When we got home that night, they told us that the hospital didn't have any for us and that there was a local shortage. They contacted other locations all day Sunday and found out they would have to drive eight hours for a pickup.

We drank the last of the frozen blood on Saturday night and Sunday. We always kept a little reserve of frozen blood in case of a delay. Thankfully the school had taken Monday off, my parents left Monday morning, and they texted us that everything had gone smoothly and they would be home mid-day on Tuesday.

They asked us to stay home from school, but both Crispin and I had tests to take and practice to go to.

"You feeling edgy? We can go home and take makeup tests." Crispin assured as we pulled into the parking lot.

"Nah, I feel a little foggy, but not like I'm going to rip someone limb from limb. How about you?"

"I think I had more blood than you did. I know Mom and Dad gave us the majority, but I think you gave me the larger amount." He said it like an accusation.

An adult vampire could live on less blood than children and teenagers. Teenager vampires were the neediest in terms of how much they drank, so The Federal Blood Disbursement allowed twice as much blood for families with teenagers.

"Keep our heads down?" I asked, getting out of the truck, and Crispin nodded, shouldering his bag.

Briar wasn't waiting for us by the entrance, but I supposed we were a little late. I would have to make it up to her. Though I doubt she cared about the book bag thing. She seemed annoyed whenever I tried to act like the doting boyfriend.

As we pushed into the school, my senses heightened with all the noise and the smells, and I felt something strain in me. I looked over to Crispin and watched as his eyes scanned the hallways, and then they stopped on something. I looked to where his gaze caught and saw Briar talking to Morgan Pope by her locker. Her arms were folded, and her eyes narrowed at him. I started to walk toward them.

"Darcy, maybe you should let her take this one alone," Crispin warned from behind me.

"I'm fine." I waved back at him.

I wasn't fine.

My nerves had gone completely rigid, and I walked faster, watching Morgan reach out and grab Briar by her arm as she tried to yank it out of his grasp. I had never known what people meant when they said 'seeing red,' but I knew at that moment. I took several deep breaths before I sidled up next to Briar.

"You need to listen to me," Morgan demanded of her.

I resisted the urge to reach out and remove his hand from her arm. I felt I might fling him into the wall if I tried. I smiled down at Briar, who made eye contact with me. She yanked away from Morgan, who let her go.

"I don't have to do shit, Morgan. You're acting like a real psycho."

"You, okay?" I asked her, ignoring Morgan altogether, not daring to look at him.

"She doesn't need you to swoop in and save her," he growled at me, and I finally looked over at him, having gotten myself to calm down.

The dude was pissed. I thought the vein in his forehead might burst and start spurting all over me. I imagined it pouring out all over his face.

Damn, I was hungry. More hungry than I realized. I needed to go home. Coming to school was a bad idea.

"I was just making sure you were okay, Briar." I ignored what Morgan said and addressed her while looking him in the eyes.

"Yeah, I'm okay."

She was not okay. Her heartbeat betrayed her, racing in her chest. Her breathing was sharp, and her eyes shifted over and over to Morgan. Despite her words, I knew she still had feelings for him. A crashing wave of jealousy flooded me, so strong I had to grit my teeth.

I needed to go home. I had been so terribly wrong.

"Whatever game you are playing with this jock can be over now. There is no way he's doing it for you. Look at him. Not to mention how you guys act together like you are afraid to touch each other."

"Shut up, Morgan. You don't know anything. Why don't you go give yourself another living room tattoo."

"Want me to walk you to class?" I asked, finally looking at Briar, who looked pissed now. "Here, give me your bag."

She handed it to me, and I mustered every drop of good fake boyfriend in me to smile at her. A small thankful look flashed across her face. The bell rang, and most students had left the hallway. I could feel Crispin watching me as he lingered.

Good. I'll take her to her class, and then we will get home.

We walked past Morgan, and I thought he might try to reach out and punch me. I was prepared for it. I wouldn't hurt him.

"I know what you look like when you like a guy Briar, I remember what your eyes looked like for me, and this isn't that."

She stiffened and stopped.

"It's not a big deal," I said low so only she could hear. "Let's get you to class. He's a tool anyway."

To my chagrin, she spun around to face him. I don't know why I thought she wouldn't. It wasn't within her to walk away from words flying like blades. I waited for the words she would throw back. She would slice his frail ego open as she turned her full figure around, and he got to watch me walk her to class. If he hadn't insulted me so thoroughly and grabbed her arm, I might feel sorry for him.

No words came from her, and when I turned to look at her with an eyebrow raised. She stepped into me and grabbed the straps of my backpack, pulling me down as she lifted on her toes. My eyes went wide as she pressed her mouth to mine.

I had never been kissed before. I had never dated, so whom would I have kissed? Briar's eyes were closed, and I instinctively dropped her bag on the floor as my arms went to her hips. Holding her in place so that she couldn't come closer or so she couldn't move away.

My brain started registering every place her body was touching mine. She was so warm, and her mouth was so soft as I kissed her back.

I was vaguely aware of Morgan swearing something, but I didn't care.

It was only Briar.

And her racing heartbeat.

And her blood pulsing through her veins.

I could hear it in my ears like a wild wind.

She made a noise that wasn't pain but more like surprise. I stiffened as her body softened against mine, and she pressed closer to me. My tongue ran along the seam of her mouth, and I nearly moaned at the syrupy taste of blood.

I was shaking as I shoved her away.

I'd bitten her.

One of my fangs had dropped down and punctured her lip. She had a euphoric dazed look on her face that was clearing quickly. An enzyme in vampire spit made the victim experience pleasure while being drunk alive.

My body raged as I pulled away from her with only a small taste. I swallowed hard as I felt myself shifting. I had to get out.

I looked up and around, making eye contact with Crispin, whose eyes went wide as they met mine. Morgan had gone. At least there was that. I backed away from Briar as her eyes cleared, and she looked at me, shocked.

Shock turned to guilt, and she opened her mouth as her apology wrote over her face. It was in response to the horror I was sure was being reported across my features. The horror that I had nearly just ripped her throat out.

"Darcy, I'm...."

"I'm not feeling well, Briar. Catch you later?" It was all I could manage before I turned and bolted for the bathroom, feeling the shift take over as my hormones raged.

I made it into a stall, locked the door, and threw my backpack to the ground leaning against the painted concrete wall. It came over me violently. If someone happened upon me here and broke into this stall, they would see four sharp fangs, and my ordinarily blue eyes shifted to red. My fists balled together as my brain supplied me with the taste of Briar Grey over and over. The slightly sweet aftertaste it had left in my mouth.

She tasted as good as she smelled.

Images of my mouth on her neck flashed in my mind as she begged me to drink more, to take more. My name fell from her lips like a caress.

"No!" I shouted, the walls echoing the anger back to me.

The images passed, and the urge to find her, kiss her, and lick away the evidence of my misdeeds fled. I was breathing hard as I willed my fangs back and did some breathing techniques my dad taught me.

I had almost killed Briar. Part of me had wanted to. More than a little part of me, and I hated myself.

At least that self. The demon that lurked within was brought out by stress and a single day and a half without the blood it needed to survive.

It didn't matter what the kids at school thought of me. It didn't matter that everyone thought I was such a nice guy. It didn't matter how many smiles I threw out or how many doors I opened. Just below the surface of who I wanted to be, lurked a monster that would kill if I let him.

Nice guy.

Nice guys don't bite their fake girlfriends.

I heard the bathroom door open. It was Crispin; I could tell by his walk alone as he approached the stall.

"Hey, Darcy?"

"I think we should go home."

"I've already got us a nurse's note." He leaned against the other side of the stall. "You alright?"

"I almost killed her, Crispin. I wanted to. I wanted to tear into her. What is she going to think of me?"

"To be honest, I think she just thinks you were freaked out that she kissed you."

"I bit her." The words came out harsh and clipped.

"You did? I'm surprised you didn't rip into her then, honestly."

"Worst case scenario, I look like a psycho boy that bit the first girl who ever kissed him and licked her blood away like some freak...."

"Best case scenario, you look like a senior who was weirded out that you got kissed by your girlfriend."

"Fuck."

Chapter Twelve

Briar

Have you ever felt like such a complete tool that it puts you in a bad mood? You want everyone else to feel like a big pile of crap too? Except in my case, I'm almost always in a bad mood at school, so the rest of Tuesday was incredibly shitty. I got written up twice for mouthing off to teachers. Mr. Gorsheld was one of them; the other was a sub teaching the AP Economics class. The class I wish I hadn't signed up for and just taken an early out every other day. I bet the sub wished I had too.

Sitting in Mrs. Sheridan's office, she sat quietly across from me as I stared at my phone screen. I had opened and closed the message app and Darcy's texts several times, wondering what the right thing to say was.

Sorry, I kissed you without permission.

Sorry, you seemed physically repulsed by it.

Sorry, I made you go vomit in the bathroom.

None of those seemed right, and, in fact, had an aftertaste of feeling sorry for myself.

The news of what happened had traveled through this school like the plague, even though only a handful of people lingering in the hallways would have seen it.

I kissed Darcy. Darcy shoved me away. Then ran to the bathroom at the speed that would make The Flash do a double take. The Booker Brothers had left school for the day. I was marooned to marinate in all the snickers behind raised hands and glances thrown my way. I think the *fuck you* on my forehead saved me from any direct comments.

"How are you doing?" Mrs. Sheridan asked.

"Really fucking great." I popped a vanilla tootsie roll into my mouth.

"Mr. Gorsheld wants you written up."

"I'll drop his damn class. He's an incompetent man with goldfish eyes and poor taste in ties. I have all my math credits anyway."

"You know the calculus will look good on your applications, and you are halfway through the year already. It would be a waste."

"If he wouldn't make his male insecurities my problem, I wouldn't have a problem."

"And the sub today? The young one? What was her issue?"

I stayed quiet, throwing a dirty look at the floor.

"There are not many students that this phrase fits, Briar, but you are truly your own worst enemy."

"Have you upgraded to a therapist? Are they at least paying you more?" My eyes slid to hers as her eyebrows raised.

I shouldn't have said it, but I couldn't take it back now or give her my sob story about all my stress. Tell her I kissed a boy today to make another boy jealous, and now I felt so sick I might vomit. No, I couldn't say that.

Because if you were going to be a bitch you had to commit.

"I think we are done here today, Briar. You don't seem in the right headspace to talk about this. My recommendation will be that Mr. Gorsheld not write you up."

I hated when people were friendly to you when you were mean to them. Like Mrs. Sheridan, like Trudy, like Darcy, my fake boyfriend, I'd scared away. I got up and nodded to her.

"Sorry, thanks."

"Don't irritate him again, Briar; pick a different teacher."

"I'll try to internalize his idiocy."

"Three and a half months, then you can harass college professors."

"And I'll be out of your hair. You'll have to find another troublemaker."

When I turned back at the door, Mrs. Sheridan almost looked like she was about to cry. Her eyes were all watery, and her mouth turned down a little.

"Don't do that." Slight horror rang in my tone.

"Go on." She waved me out, wiping her eyes, and I bolted from the room.

I made my way out of the school's entrance that dumped into the parking lot. I shouldered my backpack and walked to my car, biting my lip and wondering how I would approach Darcy.

Will he be at school tomorrow? Why do I care?

I wanted not to care. I tried to brush the feeling off as quickly as I would have last week, as easily as I might brush off any of my classmates.

But the thought of how his giant-ass hand grabbed mine for dear life as we skated around the rink at a snail's pace replayed in my mind. Or how his mouth had begun to move against mine, kissing me back.

And as I walked alone to my car, I finally allowed myself to think of the small sharp bite I felt on my bottom lip. I'd bite someone whom I didn't want to kiss too. I wasn't upset about the small swollen spot inside my lip. But then, the strongest feeling of desire and euphoria washed over me as his tongue went to where he had bitten me.

I'd been kissed before, once by a boy in middle school and, of course, by Morgan. Morgan was the first boy to make butterflies fly up in my stomach. Even though Morgan was a good kisser, it had never felt like the kiss I stole from Darcy.

When his mouth moved against mine for a moment, and I heard Morgan swear and stalk away, I felt... I don't know what I felt, but whatever it was, it made it very difficult to discard my concern for his feelings.

"Briar."

I yelled as I snapped out of my thoughts to see Morgan standing by my car.

"Fuck, Morgan, have you been waiting for me here?" I went to the passenger side and threw my backpack into the seat.

Morgan was leaning against the back of the car. His arms crossed over his black T-shirt. His dark hair was half pulled back from his face. Some of his swirling black tattoos peeked out from the bottom of his sleeves.

I wish seeing him didn't twist my insides up. The memories of his arms wrapped around me, his mouth at my ear whispering things to me about the people who passed us, were so quickly re-lived.

I wish. I wish. I wish.

If wishes were horses, beggars would ride. As my mother always said.

"We didn't get to finish our conversation before the walking PBS special came over."

I walked around my car and stepped out of his way as he reached out.

"Briar, I care about you."

I laughed as I put my hand on the handle of my driver's side door. It was the kind of laugh that came out of me when someone looked at something I was eating and asked: *can you eat that?* It was the *keep talking and you might end up missing and on late night news* a laugh. Now Morgan was doing the same thing to me that people who assumed they knew what I could and couldn't eat would do. He was giving me the same condescending *I care about your health, don't eat that cookie* tone. Except in this instance, Darcy was the cookie.

"You know I'm a nice guy, Briar. Do you think I would be hounding you like this if it wasn't important? I told Roger to back off, becasue I care about you."

"Nice guy?" I howled with laughter again. I forced the mocking pitch of it out of my mouth as I watched him get visibly irritated.

"I want what's best for you. Darcy Booker, isn't it."

"You gave up your say when you broke up with me, Morgan. I don't give a hippo's right nut what you think. Stay in your lane and out of my way, and if you ever tell Darcy Booker to stay away from me again, I'll tell everyone at school you jerk off to animal videos."

"I never took you for a liar." His face was flushed. The truth was I had no idea what Morgan watched in his *special time* in the dark.

"I'm not, but I'd make an exception for the guy who let rumors circulate that he broke up with me because I was bad in bed. I'd make an exception for you, Morgan Pope; now get the fuck off my car and stop following me around. Go find your new girlfriend."

"Darcy isn't who you think he is." His hands were raised as he backed away in defeat. "I only hope you realize it before anything bad happens."

What the fuck was that supposed to mean?

"Are you threatening me?"

"It's not me you have to be scared of Briar; it's your new boyfriend."

I glared at him as he walked away. The biggest drama queen I had ever known was a tattooed eighteen-year-old boy.

I sighed, pulling my phone out, and my heart swelled when I saw I had two texts.

One was from Trudy, which I opened first. I had traded numbers with her at the skating rink, but this was the first time we had texted.

Trudy: I got you some cinnamon bears for today's practice. You can totally still come even though Darcy is gone.

I sent her back a thanks telling her I was going to go home because I had a ton of homework. Not a lie, but not why I didn't want to go either.

I hesitantly opened Darcy's message with anxiety fueling my every movement.

Boyfriend Material: Want to come over for dinner Friday night after school? My mom is insisting she should get to meet you.

My previous anxiety of being worried he hated me washed away, and I was filled with different worries altogether.

Chapter Thirteen

Darcy

"Please don't say anything stupid," I said as I ran to answer the door.

"Me?" Crispin asked, hand to his chest, and I leveled a gaze at him as I passed.

I was nervous about having Briar over. Mom was making spaghetti and meatballs. It was a family specialty because the tomato sauce and fresh meatballs were labor-intensive. My mom didn't make it for any little thing.

I was even wearing jeans and a dark blue V-neck t-shirt instead of sweats or basketball shorts. I was wearing the cologne I borrowed from Crispin. I didn't wear cologne. I used a cedar and mint soap I liked that my mom picked up from a local store and whatever deodorant was on sale.

I opened the door and nearly laughed at her first thing. She was already leveling me with a stare that told me she didn't find me amusing.

We hadn't talked about the kiss or me pushing her away or running away. I just showed up at school on Wednesday morning and walked her to class with her backpack over my shoulder. She came to my practice on Thursday. She didn't seem bothered about it in the slightest, or I couldn't detect any nerves on her end. If I hadn't seen her nervous on our date, I wouldn't think she couldn't be anxious.

"You brought flowers." I marveled.

She stepped over the threshold, and I closed the door behind her. I took two bouquets out of her hands. One was a bundle of tulips in a waxy purple color, and the other was a smaller bundle of little daffodils.

"The yellow ones are for you." She reached down and began untying her shoes to leave them at the front door.

"You brought me flowers?" I looked at them. "I don't think anyone has ever bought me flowers."

"Well, I didn't know if I needed to bring flowers to your house since you brought them to me."

"You are never required to bring flowers, but I will treasure them until they die."

I looked her over and raised an eyebrow in surprise. She was wearing a floral skirt with a black and white floral print and a slit that came past her knee. She had a black tee tucked in that said 'peachy' in bubbly letters. Her hair was smooth like she had straightened it, and her makeup was lighter than she usually wore.

"Did you...change for dinner?"

"I took a shower when I got home from school." She brushed my question off.

"Are you dressed more...normal? To meet my family?" I pressed as she took a deep breath and gave me a dirty look.

"What does more normal mean?"

"I mean, I may be risking my life here saying this, but you look, dare I say, approachable?"

"Fuck off, Darcy. I didn't feel like getting all done up again. There was no thought put into being more normal."

"Okay."

"Don't say okay like that."

"Like what?"

"Like you think you figured something out."

She was still glaring, but the corner of her mouth had quirked up a little bit, making me flush as a smile split my face. I involuntarily thought of her mouth on mine and her hands pulling me to her.

She tastes good too.

That thought brought my effervescent feelings to a crashing halt, and I turned to lead her through the house.

"Ma! Briar brought you flowers!" I turned and led her back into the dining room, which my mom had set with the good plates. They were the ones that had no chips that we used at Thanksgiving. It was one of those occasions where everyone had two glasses at their setting.

"Oh, thank you, Briar; how thoughtful are you?" My mom rushed over to us and wrapped Briar in a hug. I nearly started laughing at Briar's expression as my mom squeezed her tight.

"I'm Katherine, of course, but you can call me Kat; absolutely under no circumstances do I go by Mrs. Booker. That is my moth-er-in-law."

My mother was nervous, and I did my best not to chuckle at her. It seemed that even though Briar was just a fake date, there was a buzz of trying to impress her permeating the house.

"I'm going to put the flowers in some water," I said.

"No flowers for me?" Crispin walked into the dining room and sat in his regular spot.

"I don't know if I even like you," Briar parried, and Crispin laughed.

I left Briar, whose eyes snapped to mine as I exited the room. She seemed to be begging me to stay, but I just winked at her. I heard

Crispin say something, and Briar responded. This could be a very long night between the two of them.

"She's cute," my dad said from the kitchen door, where his arms were crossed as I passed him and went to the sink.

I swallowed hard, facing away from him. My dad had a way of seeing right through me. I was also on edge because Crispin and I had decided not to tell our parents about me nearly ripping Briar's throat out at school. He'd promised to keep it to himself, and despite my brother's filter-less way of speaking, he was a good secret keeper. I was feeling guilty for lying to them, and I think I was a little on edge every time Dad and I were alone together. I felt like any minute, he was going to say he knew.

I reached under the sink for two vases and absently filled them with water.

My father would have been disappointed in me if he knew, and that was the worst thing about it. After trying to teach us for so long how to control our urges—teaching us ways to expel the energy and channel the hormones. They made many sacrifices to teach us how to be upstanding members of society with our disease.

And after all that, I had almost drank Briar dry because she happened to kiss me on a day I was a little hungry. Maybe they'd wasted their time.

"Darcy?" Dad questioned, and I turned, setting the flowers into the vases.

"Hm?" I asked, wiping my hands on my jeans.

"You, okay?"

"Yeah, just thinking. Sorry did you ask me something?"

"No, just saying your pretend girlfriend seems nice."

"Nice is probably the wrong word to describe Briar, but she's cool, yeah."

I walked back out through the door, and he followed me into the dining room, where Crispin had an eyebrow raised at Briar, who had her eyes half-lidded in contempt. I looked at Mom, her eyes wide but a ghost of a smile across her face.

It made sense that Crispin and Briar would be at odds with each other. Crispin was generally at odds with anyone who gave him any attitude back. Including Maisie. Crispin and Maisie were like oil and water. They were friends deep down, but if you came upon them as strangers, you might mistake them for enemies. They were constantly insulting each other.

I sat next to Briar as my mom passed the large bowl of pasta for us to self-serve. Briar said nothing except *thanks* to my mom for preparing the meal. We passed the garlic bread and the salad, and we all took a few silent bites before anyone spoke.

"So, Briar," my dad cleared his throat, and I braced myself for whatever he was about to say. "My boys refuse to explain what a fake dating relationship is. Would you be so kind?"

"It's like having a regular boyfriend, except you don't have sex or kiss each other." She looked up at my dad, challenging his question as I choked on the spaghetti I had been swallowing. My mother flushed a bit, and Crispin let out a single bark of laughter.

"Well, that's a relief." My dad said, struggling to find an answer.

"We hold hands though, and Darcy carries my backpack in school." Before taking a bite, she picked up her garlic bread and addressed him directly. "Any more questions?"

"No, I think that will be my final question of the evening."

"Briar dear, we are going to Middlewood Resort for Darcy's eighteenth birthday next week. Would you like to come with us?" my mom asked her sweetly with a tone I knew she hoped would move us past the previous conversation.

"Oh." Briar looked taken aback.

I ducked my head to hide a smile. Direct questions or accusations did not phase Briar, but kindness and politeness did. It threw her off her game, and I saw her struggle to respond.

"Mom, don't put her on the spot." I chastised.

"Oh, Dear, come if you want, no pressure."

"I'll ask my mom if it's okay," Briar said, and I could tell she was lying by how long she held the fake smile.

I wondered if Briar asked her mom's permission for anything.

"It's your birthday in a week?" Briar asked as she loitered outside her car door.

"Yes indeed." I rolled my neck back and heard a series of soft popping sounds.

"Why didn't you tell me?"

"You didn't ask, and how weird would it be for me to volunteer that information out of nowhere?"

"What do you want for your birthday?"

"For you to come to dinner with us." She let a quick breath out of her nose, letting me know that wasn't the correct answer.

"A tangible item I can wrap up for you, sweetest boyfriend ever." Her tone was full of venom and mocking; for some reason, I found it incredibly attractive.

"Something homemade."

"I'm sorry?"

"Something you made, a drawing or a painting or a piece of origami, a blanket maybe, one of the fleece ones you cut and tie together. Did you ever make those as a kid?"

"No." She stared at me like I was an alien. "Do I look crafty to you?"

"Figure it out; you asked me what I wanted."

She huffed again but didn't argue as she turned to open her door, and I stepped away from her.

"Hey, Darcy, I'm sorry." I stopped and turned back, but she wasn't looking at me. She was looking into the window of her car. "About the kiss thing, I shouldn't have done that without asking."

More guilt washed over me at her apology. I wanted to tell her that it was in no way her fault. How could she have known I would be tempted to sink my teeth into the pale flesh of her neck?

"Oh, no worries, I wasn't feeling great. I think Crispin and I had some bad sushi or something. Though it was a bit sudden, I was not repulsed by the idea of you kissing me." I kept walking away and turned to walk backward when I hit the driveway of my house. "Maybe just give me some warning next time."

"Next time?" Her head shot up as her mouth twisted into a quirk.

"Yeah, I think I would be fine with even one second of heads up."

"There isn't going to be a next time," she hollered at me as I got further away. "Why do you always do this, Darcy? Did you hear me? There is *not* going to be a next time!"

Chapter Fourteen

Briar

"That's it. I'm breaking up with him before Saturday, so I don't have to do this anymore." I dropped the strands of cord I had been trying to braid.

"You're the most impatient person I've ever met," Triana said where I had her propped up and leaning against the sugar jar. "Pick them back up and try them again. You already went to the store and got all the cute little colors that remind you of him. Super sugar sweet, by the way."

"Shut up, Triana," I grumbled at the phone, picking up the soft strands of cord I was using to make a friendship bracelet.

Triana and I had made a thousand of these in the fifth grade. She had always been better at it than I had, but it seemed I had lost the skill altogether. When Darcy said he wanted something homemade for his birthday, this was all I could come up with. Well, I thought about making him dinner too, but that struck me as more real girlfriend-ey. Or maybe making him a bracelet was more girlfriend-ey. I had no idea anymore, and I was too scared to think about it too hard.

I'd picked: a blue color that reminded me of his eyes, white for the sneakers he always wore and the truck he and Crispin drove, purple for our school's color and the basketball jersey he wore, and a sunshine yellow for his personality. With all those colors, I was trying to make a chevron-patterned bracelet, and I was failing miserably.

"I'll draw him a picture," I grumbled.

"Oh yes, your artistic talents will wow him," Triana said sarcastically.

"It's not the time, Triana."

"You called me, Homie."

My mom walked through the door at that moment, and I realized I was fucked because it meant it was late. I looked at the stove and groaned at the green blinking numbers telling me it was ten forty-three pm.

"Hey, baby girl," she said, walking into the kitchen and kissing my head. "Oh hey, Tri!" she said, getting eye level with the phone.

"Hey, River!" Triana sang back.

My mom was born in nineteen seventy-five, and her parents were major hippies. Her mom had died before I was born, and we had a few pictures with my grandpa, but he died when I was five, and I didn't remember that much about him.

"I gotta go, actually," Triana said.

"Have a fun rest of your trip," Mom said, opening the fridge and pulling out the chicken pot pie I had made for dinner.

"Love you," I said, reaching for the phone.

"Don't give up. It was a good idea. I'll text you tomorrow."

"We'll see." I hit the end button.

"Friendship bracelets? You get back into that?"

"No, it's for Darcy. For his birthday."

"Cute!" my mom exclaimed, sticking a fork into the leftovers without heating them up.

"We will meet you at the bar tomorrow for dinner?" I asked.

"Yep, a new taco truck parks in the lot every Friday, and their food is incredible. I figured we could sit outside."

"Sounds good."

"I'm excited to meet him."

"He's excited too." I rolled my eyes, thinking of the lopsided grin that Darcy had gotten when I asked him if we could drive forty minutes outside of town to meet my mom for dinner.

We had been dating for two weeks now, and I was falling into a rhythm of walking next to him in the hall, eating with his group, and sitting with Maisie and Trudy at his practices while I did homework.

I warmed up to Maisie, and I think she had been abrasive because I had been. She was very protective of Trudy, who was the world's softest human on the planet. She and Darcy were the group's sweet rolls. Maisie and Crispin were salty, mainly with each other, and Eric was easygoing and told too many 'that's what she said' jokes. The cult wasn't too evil as far as teenage cults went.

The longer I went on pretending, the more it felt like I was integrating into his life. Worse than that, he was incorporating into my life. He had come over on Monday to do homework, and I didn't feel weird having him sit on my couch, mostly taking up the entire space because he was a fucking giant. We did homework, he ordered wings for us, and we watched two rerun episodes of The Office.

Now I was making him a friendship bracelet for his birthday. I was in too far. I could admit that, but I wasn't sure how to get out and wasn't sure I wanted to go back to how it was before, when I spent most nights alone. Even when he wasn't at my house, we texted most nights about nothing, and I checked my phone too quickly when his text tone went off.

"Pie was good, darlin'. I'm going to sleep."

Mom wiped her face with a napkin and headed down the hall, leaving me alone with the demon bracelet.

"I won't bend over for you," I said to it very sternly. "You will not win."

Friday, I got out of my car and turned around to find Darcy there to walk me to class. He grinned and held his hand out for my backpack.

"I think you have a problem," I grumbled, handing it over. He pulled it up on his shoulder, bunching up his light blue hoodie, the color making his eyes look terribly spectacular.

"Don't talk about yourself that way, Briar. You are not a problem; you are a delight."

"Let's go, Moron." I trudged forward, feeling the weight of the thing I had in my pocket.

"I'm excited for tonight." He was pulling his steps back to match mine so he didn't get ahead of me.

"We are having street tacos. I guess there is a new truck near my mom's bar."

"Great! I am going to run the exercise course with Crispin at Poplar Park after school. Want to meet me there? Since you're driving, do you mind taking me home after?"

"That's fine."

"After the course, I'll rinse off at the community center quickly. So I don't offend you in your tiny car."

"I've smelled you when you've been working out, Darcy; it isn't unpleasant."

Why would I say that? What a weird thing to say.

"Well, maybe I'll just let you enjoy the aroma then."

I gave him a sideways look but kept walking as he opened the door for me, and we weaved through the sea of teenagers. We made it to my locker, which had not been tagged since the day I had waved to Darcy. I opened it to stick my stuff inside, taking out the textbook and laptop I needed for class.

"Here." Feeling flushed and bothered, I took out the bracelet I had stayed up until one in the morning making him. It had taken me a long time, but I finally got it.

"What's this?" He reached out and took it from me very gently.

"For your birthday, it's a friendship bracelet." I frowned, not liking the reaction in my chest triggered by how he looked at it.

"What do the colors mean?" he asked, turning it over in his hand.

"Nothing, they were just random ones I grabbed."

Liar, liar, pants on fire.

"Will you put it on me?" He held his wrist out, and I took the bracelet and tied it around his wrist. Not too tight but not loose enough to fall off. I brought his wrist to my mouth to tighten the knot with my teeth and fingers.

"Jokes on you for asking me to make you something. You got this shitty bracelet. Think more carefully next time."

I looked up, and my breath caught at how his gaze met mine. I wasn't sure if I had made it up, but it seemed like he was staring at my mouth before his eyes snapped back to mine and the inky look that had crossed his features for a moment washed away.

"Are you kidding?" He put his hand down and away from him like he was inspecting a manicure. "This is my favorite present I've received in a long time."

"Stop." I held up a hand.

"I'll treasure this for the duration of my natural life."

"Darcy, stop."

"I might take insurance out on it."

"I'm leaving," I said, slamming my locker and shaking my head at his smiling eyes.

"I will pass it on to my children!"

I gave him the finger as I turned and walked to class. I was too warm, too happy, and the smile that fought its way to my face was too insistent. I hated it. I hated the weak part of myself that wanted to accept his soft smile and let it thaw my chilly disposition.

Chapter Fifteen

Darcy

"What's that?" Crispin pointed to my new bracelet as we cooled down from doing the course on the baseball bleachers at Poplar Park.

"Birthday gift from Briar." I beamed, holding it up to him for him to inspect.

His eyes shifted from it to my eyes, and I could tell from the slight frown on his face I didn't want to hear what he was about to say. I stood up and walked away casually, hoping that would deter him.

"Maybe you guys should quit this thing earlier than you planned."

I ignored him going to the car as anger flared up in me.

Anger? No, defensiveness.

"Darcy." He jogged to catch up with me.

"I heard you." I opened the truck door and grabbed the change of clothes and the towel I needed to shower across the street at the community center.

"I see how you look at her. It's only been two weeks; I'm not trying to be a dick."

"Then don't be a dick. Is it hurting anything?"

I didn't bother to deny it. Not to Crispin. Not only would he see through any lie I attempted to tell him, but I didn't want to lie to him.

"It could." He followed me as I crossed a the street waving to a car that stopped for us.

"She's still hung up on her ex, Crispin; nothing will happen. This whole thing is to show him up."

"Don't fucking give me that."

"I don't know what triggered this conversation, but can we return to your preferred long silences." My voice held an edge I didn't like—a tone I was not particularly eager to take with him.

He stopped talking and said nothing the whole time we showered off and redressed. He gave me several glances but didn't try anything until we returned to the truck, and I put my towel and dirty clothes on the seat.

"Pull-up reps while we wait?" I asked, walking over to one of the stations of the park course.

It was silly to challenge Crispin to pull-ups. I was taller than he was by three or four inches, but he was broader and stronger than me.

I reached up for the tallest bar holding onto it with both hands as he walked over, and I watched his shoes flatten the green grass that begged to be cut.

"I'm just saying, Darcy, it's your first relationship. Of course, you are feeling all those puppy love feelings."

"I think you should just be quiet." The edge hadn't disappeared, and he blinked at me in surprise.

"She's not into you, she's using you, and you are falling for her. In two weeks, Dude."

I dropped my hands and stepped forward, and he stepped back. I was offended and irritated with him. He was always acting like the older one, telling me what I should and shouldn't do. For some reason, him saying Briar wasn't into me stung.

For some reason.

I knew the reason. It was because part of me wished that she would be. She would prefer my outgoing, happy demeanor over whatever vibe Morgan Pope was putting off. The past couple of days, I wished she might one day look at me like she looked at him when he passed in the hall. Like she wished I would look back at her.

Crispin's words had ripped open a shallow wound I had created myself.

"Drop it," I growled.

"Or what?" He stepped forward. "You don't want to hear it, but I'm going to tell you how it is. I always have."

He squared off with me as we stared at each other.

"Crispin, don't."

"You're too kind for her. You're too good, and she's going to shred you to pieces, and you'll let her."

I shoved him hard. He stumbled backward, and his eyes filled with surprise again and then anger. He stalked forward and pushed me back.

"What the fuck, Darcy?"

"I told you to shut up, but you can't, right? You think everyone is entitled to your shitty opinion." I emphasized the last three words by pushing him back.

He ran at me and knocked me down as we wrestled in the grass.

"This just proves my point, you idiot," he said, hitting me in the side with his elbow, and I let out a sharp breath.

"I said shut up!" I yelled, bringing my fist into the side of his thigh, and he yelled out.

I looked up and realized someone was walking toward us, but it wasn't Briar.

"Crispin, get up," I warned, trying to untangle myself.

"That's going to leave a fucking bruise, Darcy."

"Shut up and get up," I whispered, and his head turned to look where I was looking.

"Fucking, hell." I got up off the ground and held a hand out to help him.

He brushed his pants off and stood straight as Morgan Pope stopped before us.

"What are you doing here, Morgan?" Crispin asked.

"Isn't this a public place?"

"Sure, but the sign at the entrance says explicitly no weapons, and your shiny silver blades there look a little too polished for a chance encounter."

Sure, enough, on a belt looped through his dark wash jeans, Morgan Pope had two double-bladed hunter weapons strapped to his side. Hunter blades were made of steel and silver with grips in the middle that reinforced their punches in hand-to-hand combat. Silver wasn't deadly to us on the exterior, but a cut from that blade would stop the quick healing the vampirism infection gave us.

"No weapons in the park, yet two vampires can walk around freely."

"Morgan, you need to think about this; this is a public place. What? Do you plan to kill us here?" I asked, my eyes shifting from his weapons to his face.

"I have no intention of hurting you. Either of you, I can be reasonable. I'm just here to ask you to leave Briar Grey alone one more time."

"I think the obsession has hit next level. Dude, the girl has moved on," Crispin taunted, and I shot him a look. He would only aggravate the situation.

"It's my oath to make sure no harm comes to any human at the hands of one of your kind, you bloodsucking leeches."

"Ah, archaic insults." Crispin opened his mouth to say more, but I talked over him.

"Morgan, no one is hurting anyone. I wouldn't hurt Briar."

"Maybe you believe that." He reached down and unsheathed one of his blades. "That's the sick twisted thing about this progressive way our orders are moving towards. Deep down, they aren't taking into account what you really are."

"Morgan," I warned, putting my hands up and backing away.

In recent decades, the Order of Vampires Affiliation, or OOVA for short, and the League of Hunters had been working together to bring peace between vampires and hunters. For the last twenty years, more resources had become available for vampires, and the LOH had wholly banned the hunting of peaceful vampires.

"You could get in trouble for this by your people," I reminded him, reaching out to grab Crispin's shoulder.

"Maybe you threatened me."

"Morgan, we don't hurt people. We get our blood from sustainable sources; we never drink straight from humans." A sort of lie, as I remembered how Briar's blood had tasted. Just a drop, warm and delicious.

"Take care of the problem before it becomes a problem." Morgan went on stepping forward. "My father is right; these new ways will never work. You all need to be dealt with like the disease you are before you can turn into the monsters he's told me about."

There were wild vampires. They refused to drink cold blood and integrate into society. The disease gave them more strength than an average person, not much more, but it gave us a bit of an edge and heightened senses. Some vampires thought that vampirism was a mutation of superiority and that the world should accept that we were the next evolution of humanity. My parents did not hold that belief, but there were some, and their numbers weren't small, that rebelled against the decrees of OOVA.

"Morgan, please, this is not the place for this."

"As I said, you bloodsucker, I'm not going to hurt you, but if you so much as look in Briar's direction."

"You'll what?" Briar's voice came from my left, and my eyes snapped to hers. How long had she been standing there?

Her eyes shifted between us as my heartbeat quickened with the implications of her witnessing the scene before us and maybe overhearing things she shouldn't have.

But there she was, in her ripped jeans with rhinestone studded fishnets poking out through the holes, her ever-present combat boots, and a t-shirt tucked in that read 'damn' in bright yellow letters.

"Morgan, you better back your ass up with whatever medieval weapons those are because I'm going to call the police and have your ass arrested."

Chapter Sixteen

Briar

I was silent for twenty-five minutes. I watched the time count away on the digital clock in my car on our way out of town. Darcy sat in my passenger seat. His eyes kept slinking over to mine, and he was pale with nerves, but he didn't say anything to me. Though the longer I took to think, the more increasingly visibly anxious he became.

It had started with him rolling the bracelet I made him on his wrist around and had now escalated into foot tapping against the floor.

When I had threatened to call the cops on Morgan, all three of them had said no all at once. Crispin yelled at Morgan to leave as I surveyed the scene before me. My mind reeled with information. First, I walked over to see my ex advancing on the Booker brothers with a knife. On top of that, they hadn't looked that surprised. But before I could say anything, I was caught off guard by the conversation.

"Morgan, we don't hurt people...we never drink our blood straight from humans."

"You all need to be dealt with like the disease you are...."

My head spun like a bad ride at a kiddie carnival. All I had the capacity to do was tell Morgan to fuck off with his weird double daggers.

Once he had gone, I'd yelled at Darcy to get in the car. We were going to be late after all. Crispin eyed us wearily as I half-yelled at Darcy to tell him he would be fine with me.

Now here we were, sitting in my car, with my blinking at the road. Maybe there was a rational explanation. But Darcy saying he had never drunk blood straight from a human reminded me of the bite he had inflicted. Not that it caused me anger, it was just enough for the doubt to creep in on any rational thought. The Booker boys didn't date.

"Did you almost bite me that day I kissed you in the hall?" I questioned, and it came out extremely accusatory. I didn't bother to apologize.

He did wince, and I supposed that was enough, but he nodded as well.

"I did bite you," he said, and a flush of shame came across his features.

"You... do you have teeth?" I gripped my steering wheel harder. "Like sharp teeth?"

He opened his mouth to show me very regular-looking white teeth. But as I did a double take, small fangs appeared on his canines and the little teeth on the side of his front teeth. I quite nearly swerved into traffic. My chest restricted, and I fought the urge to scream. He closed his mouth and reached over to place his hand on mine, tugging the steering wheel a little back to straight.

"You don't have to be scared."

"I'm not scared. Who said I was scared?"

"Your heart is beating very, very quickly."

"Oh, you can hear my heartbeat now too?"

He pursed his lips and let out a small sigh looking out the window.

"Cheese and fucking crackers, this is...." I exhaled hard.

"Listen, maybe you don't want to talk about it, and I understand. I'm unsure what to say because I am unsure what you heard."

"How about you don't base what you are going to tell me on what I heard and just tell me the fucking truth." I ground out.

"The truth is... a lot Briar, the truth is a lot, and I don't want to overwhelm you."

"I'm pretty much already overwhelmed walking up to Morgan threatening you and your bother with a knife and then hearing you tell him you don't drink blood out of people. I'm at the edge of overwhelmed and about to jump off into hysterical, and if you don't tell me exactly what the fuck is going on...."

"Okay, okay," he interrupted me. "I'll just tell you, and then if you get too...if it gets to be too much, I'll stop."

I only nodded, not letting him off that easy.

"Crispin and I are vampires." He winced again as he said it, holding up his hands like he was unsure of something.

"Sure." I agreed for the fucking sake of it all because what else was I going to do. I had seen him grow fangs...or maybe they slid down...flipped out? No idea.

"You are either born a vampire, or you can contract it from blood-to-blood contact. It's a disease that isn't deadly but obviously has some side effects."

"Like the blood-drinking."

"Yeah, like that."

"But you don't drink from people?"

"No, never. Except when I bit you. To be fair, I didn't drink from you, but for total transparency, I wanted to very badly, which is why I ran into the bathroom."

"So, you wouldn't hurt me."

"Correct again. I was... well, there was a delay in our blood order from the hospital. I hadn't eaten, and I thought I should have been able to handle school, but...obviously, I was wrong."

"You probably would have been if I hadn't kissed you."

"Oh no, I was headed down that road when I saw Morgan grab your arm in the hallway."

"You don't like Morgan?" I was surprised because I had never actually heard Darcy say anything negative about someone.

He looked over at me with a confused expression. "Why would I like him?"

"Why wouldn't you? Don't you like everyone? You're always so nice."

"Just because I'm friendly doesn't mean I like everyone. It just makes me a better actor than you."

I scoffed, and my eyes widened as I exited the highway to get to my mom's work.

"This isn't some like prank thing? Like that one ridiculous tall guy on that one show? Like funny, ha-ha, to date the freak girl and get her to think you are a vampire?"

"I didn't want to tell you. It's much more complicated now."

"Why?" I asked, frowning.

"Well, I'll have to tell my parents, and then they'll have to inform OOVA, like the vampire government, and there is a whole process...."

"Will I be in trouble?"

"In trouble? No, many humans know about vampires; there will be a time when everyone knows, and we will have very different issues to deal with. No, not in trouble. They like to keep tabs. On the other hand, Morgan will be in trouble."

"With OOVA?" I questioned, feeling silly saying such a stupid word.

"No with..." He stopped. "That's not my side of the story, but what he did at the park was...against the rules. Anyway, we are getting off topic."

"I think we can be done," I said, taking a long breath. "I think I need a break."

"Okay." He nodded. "I will understand, Briar, if you don't want to hang out anymore. I really will if I could just... It's a lot to ask, but if you could not tell anyone."

There was a pain in his voice as he scraped the words out, and I bit my bottom lip. Of course, I wasn't going to tell anyone. Tell anyone what? My fake boyfriend was a vampire? I would become more of an outcast than I already was. Not to mention the most significant factor; I didn't want to make his life any harder.

As he talked, all I could hear was how his struggle related to my own, strangely with my diabetes. Being born with a disease caused him to depend on something to live. Blood was a little bit different than insulin, and drinking it was way more creepy than injections from my pump, but...I felt like I sort of understood. Not all the way. How could I ever? But this thing sounded like, at times, it fucked up his life...this thing he didn't pick for himself.

"I would never. I would never do that. You're my friend."

"Are we friends now?" He grinned wide over at me, and I found my gaze catching on the teeth that looked normal.

He looked so ordinary. There was nothing sinister or creepy about him—no coffin sleeping, cape-wearing, bad movie set in a castle vibe at all. He was still just himself.

My brain had not caught up, and I knew the ramifications of thinking too hard about the fact that, in the last hour, I had discovered the existence of a mythical creature would send my thoughts into a chaotic trainwreck station.

But I wanted to eat tacos and have Mom meet my fake boyfriend. So, we pulled into the parking lot, and I waited in my seat as Darcy got out and came around to open my door.

"Have you read Twilight?" I asked, and his extended groan caused me to laugh a bit.

"Please, don't; we don't have to do this."

"Am I... Your own personal brand of heroine?"

He looked down at my hand like he might reach out to hold it, but then he didn't. Did I want him to? My mind was too messy to decide.

"I have no idea what that means; frankly, I don't want to know."

Chapter Seventeen

Darcy

I know I was looking at her too much. We sat at a small table outside the taco food truck. I thought it was a card table. Easy to fold and put in the back of a vehicle.

"These are amazing," I said, polishing off my third taco.

"I agree," Briar's mom said, smiling at me.

River. She had told me to call her River. I wasn't retaining information like I needed to. I just kept looking at Briar. My eyes shifted to her. Searching for the rejection I thought would surely be coming.

After the shock wore off, it would hit. As my dad had always warned me, it would. People wouldn't understand. We would always be monsters to them If they knew what we were. And though Briar seemed okay now, shocked, but okay, I couldn't help but wait for the moment she woke up and realized what I was. What lurked beneath my easy smile?

"So, Darcy, where are you going to college?" River asked me, and Briar groaned, rolling her eyes.

"Mom." Briar took off her pump and pressed a button to check the lit screen.

"What?" Her mother shrugged, taking another messy bite of taco.

"I'm planning on going to the community college in Boon. I have a full scholarship for a two-year degree in business. Not sure what I'll use it for, but I figured thirty minutes away from home and a scholarship. I can work and save for my next move at home."

"Hear that, Briar?" Her mom gave her knowing eyes, and Briar rolled her eyes.

"I'm sitting at the same table as you."

"Smart kid, staying local."

"I'm not leaving you, Mom; I just don't know if I want to go to college."

"And you shouldn't go just to go." River used a taco to point at her daughter. "But you should think about it."

"Not now, Mom."

There was no tension in the back and forth, no actual irritation or anger. I had wondered for the past two weeks what Briar's mom would be like, and now that I had met her, it made a lot of sense. She was laid back, more like a friend than a mom. Which wasn't bad, I supposed. I couldn't imagine a mom being any other way with Briar. A strict and rigid parent might simply pass away from anger and stress at having Briar as a daughter.

Still, the question hung in my mind about where Briar's dad was. Obviously, out of the picture, Briar only ever talked about her mom. Or maybe he had died. Safer not to bring it up at all.

"Are you guys going to prom?" River asked, and Briar started choking on her taco.

"No."

"Yes."

We answered simultaneously, and Briar looked at me when she recovered from her near-death by a taco.

"I'm not going to prom," Briar stated.

"Okay." I shrugged, sitting back and drinking my horchata.

"Okay? You'll let her give up that easily?" River asked me after a bit of laughter.

"It's better not to force Briar," I said, nodding in her daughter's direction. "The more you tell her she has to do something, the more it seems she will not do it."

"Oh, my darling." River wrapped her arm around Briar's shoulders. "He's got your number; boy has he got your number."

"I'm not going to prom." Briar nearly pouted, crossing her arms.

"I won't make you." I held my hands up in surrender.

"Who will you go with then?" she asked defiantly.

"I think Kristy would be willing to go with me." I mused but only as a joke.

I would never go to any dance with Kristy for fear of giving her any lead on her interest in me. But when I looked up at Briar to share in a mutual laugh, she was not smiling. A deep frown and a narrowed gaze were what I received.

"Yeah, you should do that," she ground out, and I tried to keep a smile as I experienced her obvious jealousy. "You'll be the matching set of jock and cheerleader. Then you can take her to Forest Motel, where all the other teenagers hook up after prom."

"I've upset you," I said, still trying not to grin. Jealousy meant she cared, and my ego soaked it up.

"No. You. Haven't," she ground out, pronouncing every word as if that would convince me.

"Better to go with him to keep this Kristy girl away. It's the only solution," her mother said, seemingly unfazed by Briar's bad mood.

"I think so too." I nodded solemnly at River, who smiled wide.

"Gosh, I like this one much more than the last one. At least he has a good sense of humor. That walking cigarette advertisement had the personality of a wet pile of napkins."

"Don't you have to go back to work?"

River looked at her watch and sighed. "So, I do. You'd think I could take longer than a forty-minute break because I owned the bar."

"We can come out and do this again next weekend." I volunteered for it without thinking.

If Briar still wants to talk to me, then.

"I'd love that." River kissed Briar on the forehead. "See you tomorrow morning, Sweet Pea."

"Sounds good," Briar said, still giving me the side eye that I wasn't sure how I would get out from under.

"I'm not going to actually take Kristy to the Prom, Briar; I was joking." More silence awaited me when we got back in the car.

Thirty minutes of silence is how I paid for my joke. I didn't like long silences. I didn't like Briar's silence. I especially didn't like Briar's silence after she had just found out I was a vampire, and I made a joke about taking another girl to prom.

"I don't care who you take to prom."

If this was a narrator moment, I feel like the narrator would have said, *"Briar did, in fact, care who Darcy took to prom."*

"Okay, it seems kinda like you did care, but if you don't care, I won't be sorry."

"Good, you shouldn't be sorry."

More silence.

"Would you be upset if I went with someone else?"

"Would you be upset if I went with Morgan?" she asked, the razor-sharp edge of irritation still on her tongue.

"Yeah, I would be upset." The thought of her going with Morgan sent a flash of anger through me. Imagining her all dressed up on his arm, his stupid, ungrateful tattooed arm.

"Why?" she asked, gripping the steering wheel so hard her knuckles turned white; however, her tone was soft now.

"Why what?" I asked, knowing full well what question she was asking.

"Why would you care? Because you don't like Morgan?"

I could lie and say yes. Would it be a lie? I didn't like him, which contributed to the anger and jealousy I felt thinking of them together. But it wasn't the whole truth, and It wasn't even the majority. I wanted her to know the entire thing. Then at least, if she rejected me for being a vampire, I would know I was honest with her about everything.

"Partly, maybe."

"And the other part?" She turned her head a bit to meet my eyes.

"You want me to tell you?"

"No, don't," she said too quickly, her heartbeat giving her away, and I looked out the front window again.

"I won't, then."

Because Crispin had been right, I hated it when Crispin was right. He was always right. I was too attached to this grumpy girl with her wine-colored hair and fishnets. I was in too deep already. Looking at her then, I wanted nothing more than to feel what it would be like to kiss her without also wanting to sink my teeth into her.

Three weeks in, sitting in the passenger seat of her car, I realized I was no longer fake dating Briar Grey.

Chapter Eighteen

Briar

I had lay awake that night thinking of all the questions I needed to ask Darcy. All the questions I had about vampires.

How often do you drink blood? What happens to you if you don't? Do you usually sleep? Do you eat normal? Does different blood taste different? Have you ever bitten someone that's not me? How long have your parents been vampires? What does the vampire disease do to your body?

Question after question, I texted him as I lay in my bed with the covers pulled up around me. He responded to each one quickly with short and direct answers. I felt a little like I was still being punked. I hoped Darcy was not the sort of person to do that to me.

I had tried to ask him about Morgan again, but he had deflected the question.

Boyfriend Material: You should get some rest. It's nearly 1 am

Briar: You should also get some rest. Did you tell your parents?

Boyfriend material: No, tomorrow, dad makes waffles on Saturday, and it's my birthday, so I feel like the birthday spirit will ease their wrath.

Briar: Oh yeah, happy birthday.

Boyfriend Material: You are the first person to wish me a happy birthday.

I looked at the screen and felt a squeezing in my chest. I wish I could say it wasn't familiar, but I knew what it was. I was becoming attached to Darcy. I was growing fonder of him with every silly text and goofball smile. I had nearly sliced his head off when he suggested he would go to prom with Kristy.

Kristy, who didn't even bother to hang out with the crew anymore because I was there. Kristy, with her perfectly straight hair and nice boobs. Her petite frame and apparent crush on my boyfriend.

Fake boyfriend. I reminded myself.

Then Darcy's words came to me.

"You want me to tell you?"

I'd been too chicken shit to say yes. It was already too much with the blood-drinking, the pointy teeth, and Morgan wielding a freaking mummy blade in the park. It was all too overwhelming.

Briar: Are werewolves real? Witches? The Loch Ness monster?

Boyfriend Material: Werewolves, no...witches? Eh maybe...I've never met one, but I wouldn't be messing around with someone who said they were—Loch Ness monster 100%.

I chuckled, resting my phone on my chest. I had forgotten that I was supposed to have breakfast with my dad and his family tomorrow. Then I was still planning dinner with the Bookers for Darcy's birthday. My social tank was already empty just thinking about the kind of socializing required.

Briar: Want to eat breakfast with my dad tomorrow?

Boyfriend Material: The dad, huh? Not dead then.

Briar: I know it's your birthday, and your dad is making waffles. You don't have to.

Boyfriend Material: Do you want me to come?

Damn it, Darcy. Always asking straightforward questions and being too honest with me, giving me no room to play the reserved teenager. There was nowhere to hide from him when he was perfectly...mature about this whole thing.

Briar: Yes

Boyfriend material: Then I'll come.

Briar: The feeling... I got. When you bit me? What was that?

Boyfriend Material: An enzyme in our saliva that makes the victims of a bite feel...

His text dropped off.

Briar: An unholy amount of pleasure for just a kiss.

Boyfriend Material: I like to think my kiss was that good, but I don't know; it was my first.

Briar: No. No, stop, I was not.

Boyfriend Material: Yes indeed, Briar, you popped my first kiss cherry.

Briar: Please never speak that sentence out loud. I will disown you.

A wave of guilt crashed over me. Now Darcy would never forget his first kiss as me grabbing him by the backpack straps, trying to piss off another dude.

Worst. Fake. Girlfriend. Ever.

Boyfriend Material: What time is breakfast? Meet me at my house?

Briar: 10:45. I'll be at your house at 10:15

Boyfriend Material: Sounds good, Sunshine. Goodnight.

My heart swelled in my chest again, and I told it to fuck off.

Briar: Night weirdo

Darcy Booker didn't act like a vampire. Or how I imagined one would ever act. Vampires didn't have dirty blond hair and didn't smell like fresh soap, did they?

I set my phone on the charging stand and rubbed my eyes. I started drifting off when I heard Mom open the front door. I listened to her shuffle around for a little while before seeing her silhouette stop in my doorway.

"You awake, kiddo?"

"Yeah?" I said, though my voice was filled with sleep.

She came in and sat on the edge of my bed in the dark. She reached out and put her hand on my leg, rubbing her thumb back and forth.

"I like that boy."

"Yeah?"

"Yeah, you like him too?"

"He's…"

My thoughts wandered to what I thought of Darcy. How I had wanted him to hold my hand earlier and how I had been disappointed that he hadn't. How *I* had asked *him* if he wanted to get breakfast with my dad. I wanted to ensure his second kiss wasn't as horrific as his first. I wanted to make sure myself.

"Yeah, I like him, Mom," I whispered it. If I only told my mom, who else would know? It was just us here. My mom was like Mrs. Sheridan. Whatever I said to her would never leave this room.

"You scared?"

"Kind of, yeah." For so many reasons, she had no idea. One of those reasons was I was trying to figure out why Morgan wanted Darcy un-alived.

"Why?"

"He's so different. Goofy and sweet. He tells me things without trying to be like this… tough masculine man. He's just happy and light and…."

"And?" She prompted me when I stopped, but I couldn't think of what to say, and I was horrified to find that I was tearing up. "And you're not."

"No. I'm the dark storm cloud come to rain on his sunny day."

The thoughts began to hit that always came at night when I didn't want them. What if Darcy got tired of hanging out with me? What if he slowly began to realize I would never get any nicer? I was just a grumpy old man stuck in a teenager's body. What if he thought one day, I might be more like him and then slowly realized he was wrong?

"You know what that sounds like to me?" My mom got up from my bed and walked to the door. "Sounds like a summer storm. Not a whole lot beats a good summer storm."

Chapter Nineteen

Darcy

"You'll be back in time for dinner?" Mom questioned as I took a bite of a chocolate chip waffle.

"Yeah, Ma, breakfast is at ten forty-five. We will be back before dinner. We might even stop at the mall so I can get a new pair of jeans."

"Okay." She beamed at me. She always wanted me to wear jeans instead of athletic wear. I had only one decent pair.

"So..." I started dreading the conversation so much that I had waited until nearly the last minute.

Briar would be here any second now.

"So?" Dad said from the big stainless-steel sink where he was washing the waffle batter bowl.

"So, Briar...knows."

Dad stopped washing the bowl. Mom stopped mid-reach into the fridge to put away the maple syrup, and Crispin gave me wide eyes as he shoved a bite of waffle into his mouth.

"Nolan," my mother warned, knowing my dad might lose it.

"How?" he ground out, and I nearly flinched away from the tone. I hated when he seemed angry.

"It wasn't Darcy's fault." Crispin piped in, always coming to my rescue. At least he wasn't the one who threw me under the bus this time.

"Nobody said anything about the fault." My mom shut the fridge and came to sit next to Crispin at the bar.

She looked calm, but the worry had written itself on her features and could not be erased by her calm demeanor.

"Morgan Pope approached Crispin and me at the park while we were doing a run." I admitted.

"What do you mean approached?" Dad was scrubbing the bowl, but it looked pretty clean to me.

"He means the psycho brought two old school hunter's blades to the park and threatened us."

"He did what?" It was my mom, whose tone was steel now. When I looked up, her eyes flashed red before she blinked them away.

"Kat." It was my dad's turn to say her name in warning. "Remember what you always say; he's just a child ignorant of anything but the environment he was raised in."

"Fred Pope is a disease to this community. It wasn't enough for him to threaten us when we moved here, now he's got his kid threatening ours. I won't stand for this, Nolan; I'll call the fucking order."

The kitchen went silent in the wake of my mother's threat and her using swear words.

"Well, we have to call about Briar," my dad said, setting the bowl in the sink.

"Morgan's dad threatened you guys?" Crispin asked.

"You boys don't need to worry about that. I'm sorry I brought it up. Your dad and I took care of it. It isn't a problem anymore."

"Briar is still hanging out with you?" my dad questioned me, brows wrinkled in confusion.

"Yeah, she asked *so* many questions, and I'm not sure if the shock has worn off...."

"Have you bitten her?" he asked, and his voice wasn't mad but concerned. "You know how humans are with that."

My heart rate sped up, and I dared not look at Crispin though I knew he wouldn't give me away. I prayed that my parents would think my increased heart rate was from mild anxiety. Humans had a way of becoming addicted to a vampire's bite like a drug. It's why many people frowned on vampire and human relationships. You never knew if the human was addicted to the bite of their spouse and if that's why they stayed.

"You think she could only want to hang out with me after discovering I had bitten her?" I looked him in the face in a moment of grief.

Because while I didn't answer the question, it started the cogs of overthought spinning in my brain. Was Briar only hanging out with me because I had bitten her? Is that why she was so okay with everything because she was already...swayed.

"No," my dad said, breaking my spiraling thoughts. "Of course not, Darcy; I'm sorry, I didn't mean to insinuate that."

The doorbell rang.

"Go get her," my dad said, and I knew that meant he wanted to talk to her.

I walked out of the kitchen to the front door. I opened it, and Briar greeted me with a close-lipped smile.

"Ready?" she asked, not even stepping over the threshold.

"My dad would like to talk to you," I said, realizing how it sounded.

"Okay." She stepped through the doorway.

She wasn't hesitant. The thing about Briar was that she wasn't scared, or she was, but no one could tell. I admired that in her. I wished I could be like that.

"Am I going to be hazed?" she whispered as we made our way back to the kitchen.

"In a fashion, I think so."

"Briar!" My mom said as we turned the corner.

"Hey." Briar waved to everyone as the room slipped into an awkward silence.

Crispin poured himself more orange juice. My dad stared at us for a minute.

"So," Briar started. "Vampires, huh?"

Crispin laughed. He laughed so hard that smiles appeared on my parent's faces. He stood up, taking his juice with him.

"This doesn't seem like something I need to be a part of." He walked past us.

"Good luck, fresh blood," he whispered to Briar, who rolled her eyes.

"Crispin Grant Booker!" My mother was horrified, and I smacked him on the back of the head as he left.

"You want a waffle, Briar?" my dad asked, gesturing to one of the barstools across from where he stood.

"No thanks, I'm on my way to breakfast." She sat down, not breaking eye contact with him.

"So," my dad started.

"So?" Briar countered.

"Briar, I love my boys."

She seemed thrown off by the shift in tone and sat back. She nodded once for him to continue but gave no sassy return.

"I would do anything to ensure their safety. They are good boys."

"I know," she said to my surprise.

My mom and I watched the exchange like a tennis match.

"I want to know if you are safe to trust my boys to. Or are you going to freak out and tell everyone you know that you know?"

"And what if I did?" she asked, not maliciously but with curiosity in her tone. "What if I did tell people?"

"We would have to move, be relocated, which would be a shame because we just moved here, but it's not anything we haven't done before. The Order of Vampires Affiliation would compensate you to stop telling the story. They would compensate you well if that's what you hope for."

"I have no intention of upending your lives." she said simply. "Plus, Darcy and I are going to Prom in April, so it would be kinda a drag to find another date."

They stared at each other for a moment longer as the words settled between them. I smiled at her, saying we were going to prom. Even if it wasn't true, the words did something to my insides, and I was warm like apple cider on a cold fall afternoon.

"You'll have to forgive me, Briar, I haven't met many people like you. Can you tell me, for my curiosity, why you don't seem put off by my son?"

"I have diabetes," she said, and my father's brows furrowed. "I was born with the genes from my father's side. It didn't develop until I was five, but I didn't have a choice. There was nothing I could do to prevent it. It was just something that happened to me that changed my life forever. I live with it every day. Have to think about what I eat every day, how much medicine I have left at all times, and carry extra supplies everywhere just in case something goes wrong. I have bruises all over my stomach and thighs where I have to inject my pump sites. I wake up in the middle of the night shaky and disoriented from low blood sugar. Sometimes during the day, I develop massive migraines and blurry vision due to high blood sugar. To be blunt, diabetes has fucked my life up."

We were all silent. While I couldn't speak for my parents, I half smiled a little because Briar did not share things about herself lightly. Whether my dad realized it or not, she had given him a window into her life.

"While I know it's not the same," she breathed. "I cannot fault Darcy for dealing with something he didn't choose for himself. Nor would I want to because I know how that feels. He's never hurt me."

Lie. She's lying for me.

"Well," my dad said, resting his arms on the counter. "I think, for now, we trust you then."

"I don't think you have another choice, Mr. Booker."

Chapter Twenty

Briar

"So, Darcy, hopefully, Briar hasn't told you too many atrocious things about me."

I hesitated slightly midbite with some eggs benedict between my plate and my mouth.

The brunch place was too fancy for my fishnets and plaid mini skirt. There were crystal chandeliers and intricately carved wood table legs. Everything on the menu was at least thirty dollars, and I had like seven forks.

"Nothing atrocious at all."

"Please, call me Josiah. No need for that Sir business."

I smiled at my food. Darcy was good at lying by omission. I hadn't told him anything, so no, nothing atrocious. However, I could tell him plenty.

My father had started our meal by saying, *Order whatever you like. Don't look at the price.* Which sounds nice, but the way my dad said things like that just made me want to roll my eyes. He always tried to make everyone understand what a generous person he was. I was pretty sure generous people didn't need to say it.

"How long have you two been together?" Nancy asked.

"About three weeks." Darcy smiled at her, and I couldn't blame him.

Nancy was kind and, from what I had seen, a perfect mom to Gunnar and Zoe, who were with her parents today and not present at breakfast.

"Prom will be coming up soon. Are you guys going?"

"As a matter of fact, we are; Briar is excited," he said and turned to give me a private smile and a wink.

I was happy I invited Darcy. He carried most of the conversation and seemed genuinely pleased to do so. He left me to inhale my food and smile from time to time, answering simple questions.

"Oh, I almost forgot!" Nancy squealed with excitement. Yes, squealing like teenagers when they see their friends at the mall.

She pulled out a package wrapped in balloon paper and handed it to me.

"In case we don't see you for your birthday. Oh, open it, please." She bounced in her seat a little, so I nodded, opening the card and pretending to scan the long message she had written inside where she signed her and my father's names.

"Thank you so much." I nodded and set it down before gingerly tearing into the package and seeing two pairs of fishnet stockings. One bright purple pair and one bright pink, each studded in the cross sections with pearls. "Oh wow, these are cool, Nance; thanks."

"I told her you might not still be in the phase of dressing like...that."

"It's not a phase, Joe; that's her style," Nancy chastised as my father rolled his eyes.

I gave Nancy another encouraging smile and set the tights to the side of my plate.

"Have you gotten to meet River yet?" my father asked Darcy, and my shoulders tightened immediately.

My mother did not speak ill of my father, but my father did not share that same respect for her. He had learned that I wouldn't put up with it, so it wasn't as frequent as it used to be.

"Oh yes, we had tacos last night; it was fun. She's a doll." Darcy smiled, taking a bite of toast he had just smothered in orange marmalade.

"I'm surprised; she normally works so much; she's impossible to see."

"Which you would know because you often try to see her." I fired back, my fuse too short. Usually very short and even shorter with my father.

"No need to be defensive, Briar. I'm just saying you are alone a lot. I'm glad Darcy is around to keep you company."

My blood ran hot. So hot I could feel it in my face as I bit my tongue to keep myself from yelling in a fancy restaurant.

"I think Briar likes to be alone," Darcy offered calmly, soothing my anger. "Plus, she has Triana. She's not lucky to have me. I'm lucky she fits me into her schedule."

"That's so sweet," Nancy said, giving Darcy moon eyes.

"Yes, but a teenager shouldn't be alone that often. I'm not saying River is a neglectful mother. I would never insinuate that."

That's precisely what you are insinuating, you insufferable d-bag.

"She works a lot. She's one of those women who should have chosen her career instead of a family. Take Nancy, for example. She stays home with the kids and has her business on the side."

"I think every mom's journey is different," Darcy said in response.

"I agree, Darcy." Nancy furrowed her brows together and turned to my dad.

I stood up, sliding my chair back loudly. I could have sat silently or given him a nasty look, but my dad left while my mom did everything she could to take care of me. He got a new shiny family, and he loved to make jabs about her not being around.

We hadn't been worth sticking around for. I hadn't been worth sticking around for. Just like with Morgan, I hadn't been worth....

"Oh, not another one of your temper tantrums, Briar; please, let's sit down. I'll drop the issue."

"It's not an issue," I said through clenched teeth. "Mom works the hours she does to pay for food and medicine and health insurance since her jackass ex-husband ran out on her as soon as he found out their kid had an autoimmune disorder."

"We've been through this. There were more complicated issues than you having diabetes. It wasn't about that. I wasn't in love with your mother anymore. Also..." He stood up as well. I had always known where I got my confrontational anger from. "I have paid every penny of child support that the court made me. I never missed a payment. Your mother has sucked money away for you and the health insurance for thirteen years despite me having no custody."

"You didn't want custody. You wanted a new wife and new kids. You forget my birthday every year, for fuck's sake!"

I was shouting. He was shouting. We were shouting.

"Joe, lower your voice."

"Sir, if you are going to talk to her like that, we will have to leave." Darcy stood up next to me and slipped his hand into mine. I was shaking.

His words stung, and I wished they didn't. I didn't want them to matter because he didn't matter.

Sucked money away for you and the health insurance...

You are a burden.

"Don't stick your dick into someone if you aren't prepared to have a child, Josiah." I spat at him, tears threatening to come. I did not want to cry. "Wrap it up, at least. I know they had sex education in your school."

"You're ungrateful for everything I've done for you, and you've been sitting at this table silent like you can't be bothered to talk to any of us." He sneered at me.

"The only person at this table I don't want to be bothered with is you. I feel sorry for your kids for what a lousy father they got." I turned to Nancy. "Thank you for the gift. I do like it."

She stared after me as I pulled Darcy out of the restaurant toward the truck we had driven. He walked around and opened the passenger door for me, but before I stepped into his car, I began to sob.

It wasn't one tear down my cheek, but actual sobs making me sound like some animal as I drew in a breath, and my body shook with anger and sadness.

"Oh, Briar, oh no, don't cry." He pulled me to him, wrapped me in an all-encompassing hug, and stroked my hair as I wailed into his shirt.

Even after I was done and just sniffling, he ran his hands through the underside of my hair. I pulled away and wiped my nose on my sleeve.

"Want to go get ice cream at the mall?" He gestured for me to hop up in the truck.

"Can I get Dippin Dots even though they are wildly overpriced?" I pushed my burgundy waves behind my ears.

"If the overpriced ice cream of the future is what you want, Sunshine, it is what you will have."

Chapter Twenty-One

Darcy

Dippin Dots. I would have bought her whatever she wanted until the money I had saved doing summer jobs was nothing but a whisper in my bank account. If she looked at me with a tear-streaked face through her thick lashes and asked me for the damn tooth of a shark, I might learn to deep sea dive after I punched her father in the face. What kind of dad talked to his kid like that?

I got that the relationship wasn't exactly healthy, and Briar had been just as upset, but how he had made her feel...the things he said...I had wanted to punch him. The feeling did not come all that often, but I realized I was becoming more and more protective of Briar.

"Banana split," Briar said to the man serving the small ice cream spheres.

I paid as Briar sat on a maroon faux leather bench. I knew she was in a bad way because she gave me no fight about paying. Briar simply nodded and went to sit down. I ssettled beside her as she scooped the treat into her mouth.

"Sorry about that," she mumbled, pushing her ice cream around awkwardly. "About my dad, I should have warned you."

"It was stimulating. Got my heart rate up."

"He's just not been around a whole lot. I get upset when he talks bad about my mom."

"I get that."

"Sorry, I cried."

"You don't have to be sorry for crying."

"I got mascara and tears on your shirt."

"My mom uses good laundry detergent. I'm not worried about it."

We sat in comfortable silence as she finished her ice cream, and I watched as people walked past us in droves.

"I have to get some jeans here. Is that okay?"

"Sure." She got up and threw her trash away.

"Do you need to go anywhere?" I asked as we stared the way I knew the department store was. "Hot Topic, perhaps?"

"Shut up," she laughed.

We made it to the department store, and I went to the jeans brand I knew I liked. I also knew my size, and there was no use in trying something new if I knew these fit. I also browsed the button-up shirts. My mom would be so happy if I wore jeans and a button-up to my birthday dinner tonight. I picked up a striped white and black one with thin lines of caramel color in there as well.

"What do you think?" I asked, showing Briar. She looked around me at the other shirts and pointed to a blue long sleeve with tiny white stripes running vertically.

"Blue makes your eyes look nice."

"Oh?" I wiggled my eyebrows at her, and she frowned.

"Not like that idiot."

"Like what then?"

"If you don't pay for your shit and take me out of this department store, I'll start walking back to your house."

"Take it easy, Hot Topic. We're going, we're going." I held my hands up in surrender, but I didn't miss her pleased expression as I put back the shirt I picked in favor of her choice.

We wove through clothes and jewelry counters, trying to find a line that wasn't too long. As we walked along, Briar did what my mother did when she saw something she liked. She slowed, turned, and almost stopped but eventually went on her way. I stared at the simple black ribbed turtleneck dress with no sleeves. My dad always said to pay attention when someone did precisely what Briar had just done, and you would never be worried about what to get them for holidays.

"Briar, would you grab me a coffee at the kiosk by the food court while I check out?" I questioned, pulling out my wallet to give her some money.

"I got it, asshat," she said, waving me off as she nearly bolted for the store's exit. Briar wasn't a department store person.

I walked back to the black dress to check the sizes in confusion. I had never bought women's clothes before. But the small and the medium looked too small, so I got a large and hoped to hell the size I picked was neither offensive nor too big. I checked my price tag and sucked my breath in.

Women's Fashion. My mother had always complained.

I checked out and placed Briar's dress in a separate bag and went to find her so we could head out.

❧

We made it back to my house, and were in my room, where Briar looked over all my photographs smiling at things I'm sure I would never understand.

She had cleaned her face up in the car, and there was no evidence that she had been crying earlier.

I pulled my shirt off and grabbed the new bag of clothes, picking out the shirt she'd chosen. Ripping the tag off with my teeth, I made eye contact with Briar, who was staring at me.

"What?" I said, spitting a bit of plastic onto the floor and unbuttoning the shirt enough to slip it over my head.

"You're just changing right here?" she asked.

Was she flushed? Was her face flushed? My pride swelled in my chest, and I kept amusement from my face.

"I didn't take you for a prudent Polly." I went for the button on my jeans, and she narrowed her eyes at me.

"I'm not."

"Okay then." I was warm; I was too hot as I slid my jeans down. I was wearing boxer briefs, so it wasn't indecent, but for some reason, the way her eyes lowered to look at my bare legs and then flicked back up to my eyes made me dizzy. I slid on the jeans. I was unable to look at her as I did it. I slowed my breathing and peeled the sticker off the thigh, trying to act as if I weren't as affected as I was.

"I got you something at the mall," I said, my voice shaky to my ears as I reached for the bag.

She might not like it. She might be mad. She was always mad.

"I've had my fill of Dippin Dots," she said, as I tossed the bag.

She frowned at it, fishing the dress out.

"How the actual fuck." She held it up, letting the bag drop.

"I didn't know what size you were, so I got large because it looked right, but I don't know." I shrugged, waiting for the onslaught of swear words. Or she would tell me I was dumb or maybe ask me to take it back.

"I love it," she said, and I nearly passed out from shock.

"You do?"

"Yeah, it looks like the right size, too. I'm gonna try it on." She reached for the zipper on her skirt, and I made a surprised yelling sound and turned around.

"Who's the prudent Polly now, Booker." It was warm again. I did not turn around as she changed, even though I heard the rustle of fabric, and my teenage hormones begged me to look at the girl I had only imagined with no clothes on. Prude or not, I felt I wouldn't recover or be able to control my urge to kiss her if I saw her sliding fabric off the swells and valleys of her figure. I was just on the edge of teenage hormones just imagining it.

I needed to get it together. She was not some girl asking to be thought of like that. We were friends; she had said so herself.

"What do you think?" she asked, and I turned around.

What did I think? I thought I would be lost when she slid her combat boots on. The fabric hugged every curve of her body. It was edgy like her but also...sort of lovely. She waited for my response blinking at me with a half smirk on her face. I thanked the heavens that I would get to look at her the rest of the evening for my birthday. Quite the birthday gift; I touched my friendship bracelet absently.

"I think you're going to break my fucking heart Grey; that's what I think."

Chapter Twenty-Two

Briar

It had been eight weeks since Darcy and I had started fake dating. Five weeks since dinner with his parents for his birthday. Five weeks since I had spoken to my father. And Prom was in three weeks.

So, I was out in the next town over in thrift and consignment shops with Triana, Trudy, and Maisie. Trudy was waste conscious and had spearheaded the idea that we should all get our dresses second-hand.

"Fast fashion; you want your dress to end up in a landfill? When hundreds of wonderful used dresses need a little love?" She had said it with so much conviction that the only person still not on board was Triana. I assumed she wouldn't buy anything and end up ordering something online anyway. But she came with us and got along fine with Maisie and Trudy. That did not surprise me. Triana was an easygoing, go-with-the-flow kind of person. Out of the two of us, I was the acquired taste.

Trudy had become one of my favorites over the two months we had been hanging out. For the first month, I kept waiting for her to drop the fake pleasant attitude, but I had concluded that was just how she was.

Maisie and I got along, too, because I think we understood each other a little bit better. Maisie wasn't as… taciturn as I was, but she wasn't going to put up with anyone's shit. She seemed to genuinely not care what other people thought; if I was honest, she seemed a little braver than I was.

"What about this?" Trudy held a beaded blue gown with shoulder pads as big as a football player from the rack.

"Eighties and not in a cool way," Maisie said, shaking her head as Triana nodded in agreement.

"Oh. My. Goodness." Triana said, causing me to look up from the short jean section I had been browsing.

She held up what looked like a floor-length nightgown in a cream color with pretty lace straps and a bit of a flared skirt at the claves.

"You need pajamas?" I asked.

"It's vintage Christian Dior, Briar, you uncultured heathen." She sounded horrified.

"Well, I'm sure he got rid of it for a reason." I smiled, knowing precisely what Dior meant. I just wanted to see if I could irritate her.

She gave me a quick middle finger before Maisie inspected the tag. She whistled loudly and nodded in appreciation. "Great find, Tri. Some old-fashioned hose with the line up the back or some skin-colored fishnets and heels. Slip dresses are totally in."

Triana hugged the nightgown to her before tossing it in our cart. Maisie had already found her dress at the last store. It was pink, of course, and so offensively sparkly. It was strapless and covered in iridescent pink sequins. She said she would get some champagne-colored tulle and stitch some over the skirt and along the bust line.

So it seemed it was just Trudy and me.

"That's the one, Trudy!" Maisie said. "Go try it on!"

Scratch that. It was just me.

Trudy's dress was short and form-fitting, showing off her incredible figure. It was green velvet with some minimal beading and a strappy lace-up back. Eric would be drooling over her all night.

"Okay, Briar, you're last on the list!" Trudy announced.

"I've been through all the dresses here." I shrugged.

"What about that one." Triana pointed to a mannequin standing in another section with a witch hat on."

"So funny." I poked her ribs, and she pulled away from me.

"No, I'm serious, look." She led the group to the mannequin, and I stared at the long black dress with a boat neck and long draped sleeves that belled out. The dress was straightforward except for the heavy black fringe that lined the cuff of each sleeve.

"It's probably not my size...," I said hesitantly.

Maisie marched up to the dummy and started dismantling it. She left the poor woman in a messy pile with her witch hat and handed me the dress once she was done.

"Maisie." Trudy laughed outright, and Triana joined them as I rolled my eyes and made my way to the changing room.

I took my clothes off and pulled the dress over my underwear and bra, which were not the ones I would be wearing for this, and looked in the mirror.

"Come out and show us!" Trudy yelled so loud I was sure the entire store could hear.

I came out and gave them a sarcastic turn.

"If you don't buy that dress, I'll kill you," Triana promised.

"You would be stupid not to; it fits you perfectly," Maisie said, holding out a pair of black platform heels she must have found. I sat on the bench in the changing room and struggled into them.

When I displayed the results, Triana gave out a loud catcall, and I shot her a look.

"I told you guys this was a great idea." Trudy nodded, looking very pleased with herself.

We all piled into my car, which we had driven, and stopped at a drive-through coffee line before we headed to the bowling alley to meet the guys. I thought again how grateful I was that Triana had agreed to hang out with us. She chatted with Maisie in the back seat about the theme of what her prom would be at her school. We'd invited her to come bowling, but she had to go home. She promised to come the next time.

"Darcy is going to *DIE* when he sees you in that dress. I mean, he always looks at you when you aren't looking. But this is going to be next level."

"What, no, he doesn't." My face flushed.

"Mmmhmm... Girl, he sure does. It's adorable."

Eight weeks later, I was becoming more unsure of what to say with each passing moment we spent together. I liked him. I liked him so much more than I should have. And for the past four weeks, it felt like we were playing a game. It was an unspoken game of who could get in the most 'accidental touches.'

Brushing our fingers together or if he sat just a little too close and our legs pressed together, or my personal favorite, when he came to stand next to me, his hand resting lightly on my lower back. He hadn't held my hand again or tried to explain what he meant by *"you're going to break my fucking heart, Grey, that's what I think."*.

No, we had no mature conversation about it: only innocuous touches, flushed cheeks, and small smiles of victory. Now Trudy told me he stared at me when I wasn't looking, and I was lightheaded, suddenly wishing we were at the bowling alley so that I could see him.

"I'm telling you, pay attention tonight. You'll see what I mean." Trudy sounded so sure that I determined I would do just that.

The vampire thing hardly ever came up. I saw him drink once when we were studying at his house, and he had been a little sheepish about it as I stared at him in slight horror. But other than that and his ability to tell when I was anxious, it didn't interfere with anything much.

Other than Morgan who stared at us every time we passed like we were the offspring of Satan himself. I still hadn't gotten Darcy to tell me how he fit into all this.

But for the past five weeks, I hardly ever thought about Morgan. He was like a distant bad dream that I had moved beyond and had no intention of returning.

Chapter Twenty-Three

Darcy

Every time I looked at her, she was staring at me. And every time I caught her eyes, the knowing smile on her face grew until it was a full-faced splitting grin. It was a smile that a woman gave you when she knew something you didn't. I shook my head at her and went to throw my bowling ball.

I always threw my ball with a curve. It started on one side and hit the pins on the other while spinning as fast as one of those tops you shot off a zip-tie-looking thing.

"Dude, you suck ass tonight," Crispin said, slapping my shoulder. I rubbed where his hand made contact through my shirt.

It was fucking Briar. Every time I looked back, she was looking at me, smiling like she knew something, and sharing a look with Trudy, who just nodded. I decided to do something about it.

"Why exactly are you staring at me?" I asked, standing in front of where she sat in one of the spinney chairs.

"Why are you looking at me?" she asked, and I opened my mouth to protest, but I supposed the only way I would know she was looking at me was if I had been looking at her.

"Yeah, Darcy, why are you staring at your girlfriend?" Trudy added in, and I saw that I was outnumbered, so I backed away with my hands raised.

"Hey ladies, take it easy; I'm just out here trying to play ball."

"You should stick to basketball. We are kicking your guy's asses." Briar smiled at the scoreboard, and I groaned, looking at the boys' team score. The girls were murdering us, which means we'd owe them pizza at the end of this.

"It isn't over till it's over," Crispin said, stepping back from his turn.

"Sometimes it's over before it starts; you don't look like you've bowled a day in your life." Maisie mocked Crispin, who leaned over the ball return and narrowed his eyes.

"Too bad they didn't have a pink ball for you, Princess."

"Too bad they only hand out the little kids' six-pound balls to kids under ten; it seems like you could have used one."

"Break it up. Keep it clean, keep it clean." I joked as they locked eyes for a few more seconds before breaking apart like shrapnel.

I adjusted my brimmed trucker cap and nodded for Eric to take his turn.

We waited for pizza at the place next door to the bowling alley. Some of us were at the table, and some of us were off in the small arcade intended for children. The girls talked about Prom and their dresses and told the boys what they needed to order to match.

Briar just said my dress is black, as she typed some numbers into her insulin pump.

"Think old-school Hollywood." Trudy helped me out as I watched Briar walk to a pinball game.

"Got it. Any ideas on flowers for a corsage, Tru?"

"Oooh," my friend said from across from me, leaning on her hands. "Maybe something dark for her. Dark roses or maybe some dark dahlias. You know, because of her color palette."

"You're the best, T." I held my fist out, and she bumped hers into mine.

"I got you," she said, leaning back to discuss corsages with Eric.

I looked at Briar playing Star Wars Pinball, and she was not looking back at me for the first time that night. I thought it was a shame because a little thrill surged through me when her eyes met mine.

For the last few weeks, I had been driven as close to insanity as I ever had been. Between the looks we passed each other and the late-night texts, I was starting to fall in love with Briar Grey. Just like Crispin had said I would.

Scratch that; I was most certainly in love with her. I didn't know what love was precisely, but I thought about her all the time, and when we shared our little *touching-on-accident* moments, I felt like my chest was going to cave in...among other reactions to other body parts, but I wasn't going to be gross about it.

I got up as the pizza came out to tell her to eat. I walked over as she slid a quarter into the machine and looked at me.

"Pizza's ready," I said, smiling.

"Sounds good. Just one more game."

I watched as her ball loaded, and she shot it around as it hit, and little lights and bells went off.

"You're making me nervous watching me; I was doing much better before you came over here."

"Why am I making you nervous?" I chuckled, and she gave me a side-eye.

"You're doing your handsome giant thing where you stand next to me, like a lurking presence."

I stepped behind her for reasons unknown. Maybe it was the overalls and the pink fishnets. Maybe it was because she called me handsome. Perhaps it was that she had caught me staring at her at least fifteen times at bowling.

Whatever it was, I closed in on her putting my hands over hers on the side buttons, and heard her breath quicken and her heartbeat start to increase. It was an unfair advantage for me to hear how my proximity affected her. I could tell her it did the same to me.

"What exactly is a handsome giant thing?" I bent my head to say it quietly to her.

"You know…" Her voice was shaky. I wanted to kiss her so badly.

I reached over, released the ball, reloaded into the side, and pressed over her fingers to play the game.

"I'm doing just fine. Maybe you just suck at pinball."

"Maybe you just suck in general." She breathed out.

Her proximity was affecting me. I felt drunk, like the time I had drank all that spiked tea at my cousin's wedding on accident.

"Was that a vampire joke?"

I bent down and kissed her neck, and she took a sharp breath. Her head moved ever so slightly to allow me more access. My self-control snapped with that single act, and I put my hands on her hips and spun her around.

I reached up to turn my hat around backward as she stared at me, her wide eyes tracking my every movement. My hands settled back on her hips, and I pulled her closer.

"I'm going to kiss you now, Briar. I've just about had enough of how your fingers brush against mine, while I haven't been able to do anything about it."

"Kiss me as your fake girlfriend or something else?" she asked, staring at my mouth. She was asking too many questions.

"I'm done with fake, Briar; I don't want to be your fake anything anymore."

Her eyes went wide. As I bent lower and her mouth opened slightly.

"Wait," she ordered, so I hovered over her lips with my last bit of control.

"Not here, in front of everyone."

"Who cares? You don't care what people think." I pulled back a little and raised an eyebrow.

"No, it's not that; I don't..." She hesitated. She did it when she thought what she was saying was dumb.

"You don't what, Sunshine?" I asked, pulling back another inch, giving her space.

"I don't want it to be like a show. I don't want it to be for anyone else."

"Let's go eat some pizza," I answered her, my chest restricted with feeling.

"Okay." She nodded, taking my hand in hers.

"This just means you never know when the kiss is coming," I warned her as we walked to the table.

"You don't know when it might be coming either, Booker. Don't get too cocky. I made the first move once and could do it again."

I sat down to eat, grinning like a fool.

Chapter Twenty-Four

Briar

"How could it possibly need to be preauthorized by my doctor? She's the one who wrote the damn prescription?" I rubbed my temple with my thumb and forefinger.

"Your insurance changed its policy; they need preauthorization and sugar logs to approve your insulin usage." The tech looked a little afraid I might punch him.

I wouldn't. It wasn't his fault.

"It's the same prescription I've picked up before. It's the same insurance. They should have all that information on file."

"I'm sorry, Miss, but they are requesting more information before they'll fill it."

"Okay, well, my problem is I called this in a week ago. Having a week's worth left, I had to call and remind you to check your voicemail for the refill request, and now I have one day of insulin left."

"Yes, Miss."

"And it's Friday."

"Yes, Miss."

"So, you requested more information from my doctor today, but their office is closed today, and they won't be back in the office until Monday."

"Yes, Miss."

"So, my problem is, now that you waited until I came to pick this up to send it to my doctor, I will have no insulin for, best case scenario, two days, worst case up to a week."

"Yes," he said as I blinked hard, willing the angry tears not to come forth. This wasn't altogether unusual.

The doctors blamed the pharmacy, the pharmacy blamed the doctor, and the insurance had us all dancing on puppet strings as we did the dance they wanted us to so that I could get the medicine that kept me alive.

"What is the cash price for the smallest amount you can give me without breaking a box?"

"Four hundred and thirty-two dollars and sixty-eight cents," he said after doing some math.

I took a long breath and took out my wallet, pulling out the credit card my mom had given me for emergencies. I paid for the cartridge of insulin and snatched the card back from the tech with too much force, grumbling under my breath.

I walked to my car and cried by myself. It was just me and my expensive ass medicine.

Briar: I had to pay cash for my insulin because of an insurance issue.

I waited for my mom to respond as my anxiety ate away at me. The last thing she needed was a five hundred dollar credit card bill.

Mom: No worries, Pumpkin, You wanna shoot me a picture of the receipt so I can submit it to the insurance later?

I sent her the picture and a thank you before pulling out of the parking lot.

I was bitching about the situation to Triana as we carried my mattress downstairs to make a rom-com movie-watching fort for the weekend.

I felt like a neglectful friend for the past weeks. If I wasn't hanging out with Darcy, I asked Triana if she wanted to hang out with the group. She had made a passing comment about not getting quality time, and I decided it was time for a best friend's weekend.

No boyfriend, or fake boyfriend…whatever. No new friends. Just me and Triana, watching all of our favorite 90s rom-coms, eating too much popcorn, and ordering Chinese food.

"You know this may be one of the last times we do this for a while," Triana said, grabbing kitchen chairs to drape sheets over.

"Why do you say that?" I asked.

"Well, it's almost April, schools are over in a month, and then I'm going to Spain with my mother for a month over the summer. Come back and get my shit to move to California to go to school."

My stomach dropped.

"Yeah, I guess so."

What was wrong with me? Was I pmsing? Why did I feel like crying again?

"You fill out that application for the electrician apprenticeship yet?"

"Yeah, I have an interview the first week of May. The company has some sort of contract with the county. They picked two kids out of the graduating class this year to train."

"You excited?"

I shrugged, still thinking about her earlier comment. Triana would live with her cousins in California, going to the same college as her. California meant I would never see her.

"It'll be fine, B," Triana said, lining the chairs up, and I walked over to the Chinese food menu hanging up on the fridge so we could order.

"What will be fine?" I asked casually, and she rolled her eyes so big I thought they would roll right out onto the floor.

"So, you and Darcy? Official?" She changed the subject to something I didn't want to discuss.

"I don't know. We aren't what we were, but we aren't...." I trailed off, not knowing the answer. "Chicken chow mein or veggie?"

"Well, has he kissed you for real or what? I mean, other than that unfortunate incident where he nearly vomited from your kiss."

I scowled at her for bringing up the memory. Since I couldn't tell Triana that Darcy was a vampire, I couldn't correct her.

"No, he hasn't."

"Scarred after than first incident, poor boy." She sighed, and I looked around for something I could throw at her.

"Chicken chow mein, eggrolls, and orange chicken. And we are watching "She's All That" first because Freddie Prince Jr. in the 90s is the love of my actual life." She went down the hall, I assumed to get a sheet, and I punched the Chinese food place's number into my phone.

When we had eaten ourselves into food comas and were halfway into "Never Been Kissed", I scrunched my face at the screen.

"Isn't it kinda ick because he's totally into her before he knows she's not in high school?"

"It is kinda creepy. But Drew Barrymore can do no wrong."

"Do you like Darcy?" she asked out of nowhere which was very much like her.

"Fucking hell, Tri."

"What? I want to know, and you've got the details locked down like this is a national security matter."

Because.

Because of so many things, I was worried that he wouldn't be allowed to date me because of vampire stuff if we weren't fake dating anymore. His parents wouldn't let him, or the order of the vampire, or whatever it was called.

I liked him, and that was the whole problem. I did not want to get attached to people who might not stick around. I was not a creature of change.

"Yeah, I like him."

"Like him, like him?"

"What are we eleven." I huffed out, looking back at the screen to avoid her eyes.

"You liiikke him, you wish he'd kiss you," she teased in a sing-song voice.

"I literally hate you so much."

"Well, I like him," she said, sitting back against the pillows with her hands behind her head.

Chapter Twenty-Five

Darcy

"I have something for you," I said to her as her face scrunched over the math problem. I had done the problem, and she kept getting different answers than I had, and she was now reworking it for the fifth time.

"I'll figure the damn problem out on my own, Darcy," she grumbled, not even looking up at me.

But the thing I had for her was not a solution to a math problem. It was a ring, not like *THE* ring, just a cheesy little ring I had ordered online. Sterling silver with a sun on it to ask her to be my girlfriend for real. It was cutesy and ridiculous, and she would probably mock me for it, but she was at her cutest when she made fun of me, so, win-win.

"No, I know better than to offer my assistance a third time."

Our thighs were touching where we were sitting against my bed. Shoulder to shoulder doing homework, it felt like it was supposed to be like this. Like I had always been meant to do my schoolwork next to her with her hair in a messy bun. Smelling like a damn miracle. I wanted to lean in and press my nose to her neck every time she moved. A little to smell her and a little to hear the way her breath might hitch if I did it.

I lifted a bit and took out the ring feeling a little silly and a little warm.

"Will you, Briar Grey, be my not-fake-at-all-but-in-fact-very-real girlfriend?"

She stared at me as an array of emotions crossed her face, but it ended in disgust. She reached out quickly to snatch the ring from me and inspected it before shoving it very unceremoniously on one of her middle fingers.

"Why are you this way?" she asked, rolling her eyes and looking back down at her textbook.

I didn't care what she did because Briar had just agreed to date me, and I was happy as a clam.

"We can't tell my parents is the only thing," I said.

"I figured that."

"Crispin will know."

"How, if you don't tell him?"

"Crispin thinks he knows everything, and unfortunately, eighty-five percent of the time, he is correct."

"He won't tell?"

"No," I assured her as she looked down at the ring and twisted it with her fingers.

When I looked back at her face, she was wearing an absent sort of smile that was my undoing at that moment.

I leaned down to press my mouth to the hollow of her throat. I had barely grazed the pulse point I could now hear hammering away when she shrieked and pulled back from me. She fell backward on her elbows and scooted back.

"What are you doing?" she demanded, her eyes dipping to my mouth.

"Where are you going?" I questioned, moving our school stuff out of the way as I pursued. She just stared as I positioned myself over her. "I told you this could be coming at any time."

"I don't... maybe don't...." she said breathlessly as I leaned closer.

"You've changed your mind. You don't want to be my girlfriend."

"No, I haven't changed my mind."

"You don't want to kiss me then?"

"I, no, that isn't...no, that's not what I mean."

"Your heart..."

"Don't say it." Irritation crossed her face.

"I'm just saying you could be excited, anxious, or scared." I moved a lock of hair from her face as she laid back on a pillow.

I reached up to run my thumb over her jawline. "Are you scared of me, Briar?"

"A little, yeah." I stopped moving my thumb, and my eyes slid to hers with worry in my chest, but I saw the realization cross her face as her expression softened.

"Not like that." She reached up and wrapped her hands around my neck, pulling me back to where I had been. "Not like that, Moron."

Her face was flushed, and her eyes didn't falter from mine.

"I'm ...firstly, I've not kissed very many people. It may not be terrific."

"I've only kissed you, so let's take that argument out."

"I'm afraid I like you," she said like a confession; she whispered it.

"Well, I would hope so." I smirked a little enjoying the way every press of her skin felt against mine.

"Which is fine for you, but the thing is, I'm not very likable. I don't know if you noticed, but I'm very grumpy."

"I like you grumpy."

"I'm argumentative and always saying things I shouldn't be saying."

"I like that too."

"For now, but what if one day you are at college with some hot vampire chick who is nice like you and...."

So I kissed her because it seemed like an excellent response to the ridiculous things she was saying. Because right now, in my state of mind, there would never be anyone but her. Maybe it was easy to say at eighteen, but everything she had just told about herself as a negative I fucking loved.

Her mouth was warm and soft against mine. She made a surprised noise, but her hands threaded through my hair at the base of my neck, and she opened her mouth to deepen the kiss. Whatever aching chest I had experienced over the last few weeks exploded within me as it cleaved open, all warmth, light, and Briar.

There were no feeding urges ruining it. No worries, I would hurt her. I was just content to experience how her mouth reacted to mine as we found a rhythm that worked for us.

I broke away to pepper her face with kisses as she laughed. It wasn't a laugh I had heard. It was light and happy, and I would bottle the sound if I could. I kissed her neck.

"Darcy." She took that inhale I had been craving to hear, and I kissed along the edge of her v-neck collar.

"What if your parents come up here?" she asked, fingers running through my hair. If she wanted me to answer her questions, she would have to stop that immediately.

"Can't talk, too busy." I kissed her again, and she pushed me up slightly.

She reached up to touch my lip, and I felt with my tongue that my fangs had descended. Her finger slid across to the other side, curiosity filling her gaze.

No one had seen me like this, and I'd always imagined a girl would be...grossed out or horrified. Briar only gave me a half smile, causing my lovesick stupor to increase.

"Just don't bite me again."

I bent lower, pressing my face to her throat once more. I opened a little and scraped my fangs lightly against her, careful not to break the skin. A shiver flew through her as I pulled away. I felt my hand shaking. I had meant to tease her, but it seemed I was as affected as she was. She looked up at me with an evident desire that fed me and the monster that lurked beyond.

"I promise you'd like it.

Chapter Twenty-Six

Briar

My sugar got low in the middle of class, and I tried to hold out until the end, but my heart was in my throat, like a pounding in my head, and I got shaky as I felt like slumping over to take a nap. If I did, it would be the last nap I ever took. Mostly kidding; the paramedics would probably get to the school in time... probably. That was if some moron didn't assume I needed insulin while my blood sugar was low.

Darcy's eyes had been on me from where he sat since my heart rate started to increase. I respectfully opened my backpack, pulled out a can of pineapple juice, and popped the lid open. I still got a look from Mr. Gornheld, but he continued teaching.

After the juice brought my sugar up, I sat in the math class as my least favorite teacher droned on. I lightly tapped a metallic sharpie against my composition notebook to not anger him. I was on a streak of not being sent to Mrs. Sheridan's office.

Darcy reached over and snatched the pen from me. We had not always sat next together in this class. Sure, we had always been in the same class, but three weeks ago, he had asked Janene Kay to move to his seat in the back so he could sit next to me, and the girl tripped over herself to do it for him.

So now, we sat next to each other, and Mr. Gornheld was looking for a reason to separate us. So, when he grabbed my pen, I didn't throw a fit like I wanted to; I just gave him a sideways look.

He slid my composition notebook over to himself and uncapped the Sharpie, giving me a wink. He scribbled something and covered it with one of his hands. So I couldn't see it until he capped the pen and slid the notebook with the pen on the top back to me.

I looked down at it with an eyebrow raised and read:

Hey, I think you're cute. Wanna eat lunch with me?

Below it, he had drawn a heart with an arrow through it and B+D on the inside of it.

I shook my head, rolling my eyes and looking forward. He was nothing if not persistent. His finger tapped lightly on the corner of the journal until I turned to look back at him.

He dipped his head and cocked an eyebrow like he was waiting for an answer. Like we didn't eat lunch together every day. I nodded and flicked a hand up to say: *of course, moron.*

His signature grin came over his face as he stole a quick look at the teacher, who had his back turned at the board. He leaned over and kissed me quickly as the class erupted into giggles and mocking cheesy sounds. Darcy was sitting back in his upright position before Mr. Gornheld turned around, and when he demanded to know what the commotion was, no one ratted us out.

Darcy slipped his hand under the desk and squeezed my fingers once.

❦

"I've never really asked how dating my cousin was," Maisie reached back and took lemonade-filled licorice from Trudy.

We all watched the game in the little corner that we had claimed. We all wore the team's colors, and Trudy had painted Darcy's number on my cheeks. She had Eric's to match, and Maisie had gotten hearts since she was not dating anyone.

"Probably because it would be a bizarre conversation, Maisie, and you shouldn't ask." I rolled my eyes as I tracked the game with half my attention.

Unfortunately, I learned a lot about basketball while hanging out with Darcy. I now understood what was going on, but I was not happy about it, and if anyone asked, I would deny it.

"So, how was it?" She ripped off a chunk of licorice with her teeth, unfazed by the look I was giving her.

"It was fine," I said, shaking my head.

"Really, because he's always been kinda dick...."

"He was kind of a dick, but I'm kind of a dick, so I thought that's what I wanted."

"No, you're not a dick, Briar." She shook her head relentlessly with her gaze upon me. "You want to be a dick. You want people to think you're a dick, so they'll leave you alone. But you aren't, not deep down."

"How much do you charge for these therapy sessions? Because bitch, I feel like a new person."

"You're just mad because it's true."

I stared at her opened-mouthed as Trudy giggled and covered her mouth with her hand when I looked back at her.

"How do you feel about Darcy and Kia being prom king and queen?" Maisie prodded some more, and I swear my mouth opened a little at her insistance of asking me uncomfortable questions. The FU on my forehead did not work on her.

"Why would I care about that?"

I did care about it a little, but it was a stupid thing to care about. Prom king and the queen was a popularity contest, and Darcy was the sweetest new boy in school. Kia was a nice girl, editor of the yearbook, and an Ironside socialite. So, it wasn't all that surprising that she won either.

So why did it bother me? I wasn't going to think about it because I didn't want to deal with the nagging in my gut. I knew I shouldn't be bothered, so I held onto that thought. And I said it to myself every time someone brought it up.

You aren't upset. If you are upset, you are stupid. Shove it down.

"It would bother me." She shrugged.

"Well, they don't call you the princess for nothing." I jabbed back, but it was wrong. It didn't sound like a joke, and my words had a raw edge.

Maisie gave me a knowing smile and turned back to the game, leaving me irritated.

Darcy had asked at least a dozen times if I was sure it was okay. He told me he would bow out if it bothered me even in the slightest. Of course, I had acted like he was stupid for even asking. Even though he would understand, he wouldn't even make me feel silly.

But I didn't want him to understand. I didn't want to be that girl that cared. The girl that cared so much about...him? Us?

This is precisely why I didn't think about my feelings because I was too stupid to even sort them out myself.

Chapter Twenty-Seven

Darcy

"You're taking Maisie to prom?" I asked.

"Yeah, we are kinda the only ones without dates, so it seemed...." He shrugged, not finishing the sentence.

"Makes sense." I paid the total on the register and thanked the woman behind the counter as we left the shop.

We rented suits from a local place for prom, and each picked a tie out of my father's massive tie collection. Crispin's was a blush pink bow tie with polka dots, and mine was just a plain black silk tie, which Briar said would match her.

"You think it's weird? Me taking her?" he asked as we climbed in the car. I was careful not to put the suits in a way they would wrinkle.

"No, why would it be weird? You guys are friends. You do always seem to be playing some back-and-forth tennis match no one can see but...." I shrugged as I started the car. "I don't think it's weird. The pink tie makes much more sense now."

"The girl likes pink. Good thing it brings out my natural good looks."

I rolled my eyes as I drove us to the florist to pick up the corsages. Crispin was the handsome one between us, and I knew where he had gotten it. He had some of his father's features, a strong jaw, and blond hair, but his "prettiness," for lack of a better word, was from his mom, Liza Hillbrand.

The Hillbrands were like Vampire Royalty, and Liza was called the Vampire Princess in the states before her parents disowned her for marrying Matthew. According to Dad Liza's parents were wealthy, and her father, Crispin's grandfather, sat on the council. They had never even bothered to reach out to Crispin his whole life. Aside from taking Mom and Dad to court for custody, even though Liza and Matthew's will was clear. It pretty much made them shit people in my book.

Though I supposed if Liza was the vampire princess, it made Crispin the bastard vampire Prince, which suited him well.

"Where should we eat Saturday? Everywhere in town is always crowded, and I don't want to deal with that."

"I thought we'd get some stuff and picnic at the gazebo in the middle of town. I don't think anyone else will."

"A picnic?" He raised an eyebrow at me. "You realize the girls will all be wearing fancy dresses...."

"There's a table under the gazebo, asshat."

"Okay, okay, you're right. I said to avoid the crowds, and my brother recommended a picnic. How romantic will that be?"

"Do you need a romantic dinner for you and Maisie?" I teased him, and he leveled me with a glare. "It will be romantic," I assured, because this was my first and last prom, and I had it all planned out.

"All right, you'll let me know what we need to do."

"It may involve getting up early and driving to Portela."

"That's an hour away." He groaned.

"I'll buy you a coffee."

We walked into the florist, and Meg smiled at us. She was Mom's friend and owned the only flower shop in town, so prom season was very good for her.

"How are my favorite boys?" she asked, already walking into the back cooler to get our items.

We had corsages for our dates, and we had both opted for no boutonnières. Instead, we pulled some money together and got our mom an extravagant bouquet. We both agreed she had seemed kind of off the last couple of weeks, and we thought it would cheer her up.

I hadn't told Meg what I wanted because I still had no idea after Trudy's help. So instead, I just described Briar to her over the phone and told her she was wearing a black dress. Meg said she would handle it.

She did, in fact, handle it.

She brought out our corsages. Maisie's was three champagne-colored roses, baby's breath, and some soft velvet leaves. "Oh yes, that looks like her," Crispin said as she slid Briar's over to me.

It was simple, three orchids in the darkest purple I had ever seen with minimal dark leaves complimented by black satin ribbon.

"What do you think, Darcy?"

"It's perfect, Meg, thanks."

Mom cried about her bouquet when we brought it home, and she made us try our suits on even though she would see them again the next day. She was a sobbing mess as she blubbered something about us being grown up and looking so handsome.

Dad came in and his eyes went wide as if he had stepped into a war zone. Crispin and I both shrugged, and Dad just nodded.

He ordered pizza, and we all drank root beer floats on the large living room sectional and watched Casablanca. Mom cried throughout the ordeal but swore they were happy tears.

It was late when we all finally trudged off to our rooms.

"Boys, the OOVA auditor will be here on Sunday at nine-thirty. You both need to be awake and showered."

Crispin groaned an acknowledgment, and I said, "Okay, Dad."

OOVA sent a sort of social worker out to every registered vampire home twice a year. Like a checkup to ensure you didn't have any literal dead bodies or blood servants hanging around your house and that you weren't stockpiling blood. They would ask us a few questions and be on their way, but it was always awkward.

I lay awake in bed thinking of biting Briar. Biting a human was a violation, and I should have reported it to OOVA when it happened. Or told my parents and they would have. I doubted it would come up, but my anxiety played the worst-case scenarios in my mind for an hour before I could finally sleep.

Chapter Twenty-Eight

Briar

I watched as Maisie put contacts in her eyes, which always freaked me out. She blinked up into the bathroom light a few times, wiping away some stray tears, and turned back to me.

She was a comical sight, or at least by my standards. She was wearing one of those "I just killed my husband" robes in pink satin; the sleeves and hem were lined in feathers.

Trudy and I ended up at her house to get ready for prom. House wasn't exactly the right word; it was like one step down from a mansion. We'd had to drive outside town to get to it, and the house had a large iron gate Maisie had to buzz us into. The bidet I sat on looked like it cost more than me.

I felt very out of place in my black ripped shorts and shirt. Especially because Trudy had gotten her makeup and hair done and gone off to get us all coffee. So now I was alone as Maisie rolled the hair out and applied a light shimmer to her eyelids that made her brown eyes sparkle.

"What do you want to do makeup-wise?" she asked, adding the final false lash to her left eye before turning back to me.

Her usually loose, wavy hair had been straightened and perfectly framed her heart-shaped face.

"I'll just let you decide, don't make me look like a clown." I shrugged one shoulder as I studied the open shower with more buttons than my car.

"May be hard, given the canvas." She smiled at me in the mirror, and I rolled my eyes.

She brought me a beautifully kept makeup bag and set it on my lap. My makeup was in a plastic grocery bag; my brushes were all mixed in a cat mug. But Maisie's were rolled out on the counter in a leather bundle like a painter kept their paintbrushes in.

She instructed us to just come with foundation and nothing else. I might have found it bossy if I cared more about makeup. If I was honest, I was relieved not to have to be in charge of it.

"So, your family has a bunch of money or what?" I gestured around.

Her mouth quirked into a smile. "My parents have a lot of money, yes."

"Does this play into your nickname in school?"

"I suppose, though I think it's mostly that I'm small and I look like a bubble gum advertisement."

I laughed, and she smacked me on the forehead with a soft brush. "Stop moving, idiot."

She finished some soft makeup with a sparkle at the inner corner of my eyes and some tiny fake lashes, which still felt stiff and heavy. She pulled a plum lipstick out in a rich gold tube. She applied it and stepped back, admiring her work. She handed me the lipstick.

"It's never looked right on me."

She pulled the rollers out of my hair and brushed and sprayed until my freshly dyed burgundy locks were where she wanted them.

"You know Crispin and Darcy are vampires, don't you?"

She asked the question so casually that I quite nearly answered her. I caught myself and forced a snort out. My eyes met hers.

"I know, you know, it's fine. We don't have to do the whole 'vampires aren't real' thing."

I didn't know what to say. I wanted to ask how she knew, but that would give too much away. So, I didn't say anything, just stared up at her from the toilet.

"My cousin…well, my cousin and I…let's start again." She took a deep breath. "My cousin and I come from a long, old line of vampire hunters. The idiot told everyone in the family about his run-in with the boys at the park. He was proud of himself."

Still, I said nothing but all the information Darcy refused to give me started to piece itself together.

"Morgan, his brother, and my uncle are… well, they are old fashioned; they hold to old thoughts, old ways. Does that make sense?"

"No, no sense at all," I said very seriously.

She chuckled nervously. It may have been the first time I had ever seen her nervous.

"No, I suppose it wouldn't. Things are different now; my parents are different. They don't think vampires are the monsters that hunters once thought they were… we are trying… we believe…."

She was uncomfortable, I was uncomfortable, and the air was stuffed with it between us.

"I just mean to say Darcy is a good person, and I admire that you don't think he's …gross or anything."

"Do they know that you know?" I asked finally, after letting her sit silently, probably a bit longer than necessary.

"Maybe, it's kinda an awkward thing to bring up. Hey, I come from a family famous for killing your kind, but I think we could all have world peace." She braced her arms on the counter and let out a long breath. It was the most emotion that I had seen her express, and for a moment, the layers of her social mask peeled back, and I saw the teenager beneath.

"Well, that seems like a you problem. Hope you figure it out." I stood up and patted her on the back.

"Heartless asshole." She huffed out a laugh.

"Uppity bitch," I fired back from the bathroom door.

"Where are my girls at?" Trudy shouted from somewhere in the maze of the Pope's house.

"Let's get dressed and meet those idiots," I said, and Maisie nodded in agreement.

Upon my mother's insistence, I took one thousand pictures of the three of us as she gushed over everyone. Trudy made us make a TikTok video I didn't understand, and Maisie made herself another espresso on top of the coffee Trudy got for her. She also went outside, and we all sat on the porch while she smoked two cigarettes out of a dark green American Spirit pack.

We all piled into our cars to meet the boys at the gazebo in the middle of town for some surprise they had put together. I took a picture of my ankle in the platform, heels looking pale against the black-on-black, and texted it to Darcy.

Briar: in olden times, this would qualify as a very suggestive photo.

Boyfriend Material: Still qualifies. I'm an ankle man myself.

Briar: Freak.

I smiled, tossing my phone into the passenger seat on my way to take part in a teenage rite of passage I once thought I would never attend.

Chapter Twenty-Nine

Darcy

I nervously fiddled with the fake candles as the sun dipped down to kiss the hills. It was a great evening. The sky was purple, and there were very minimal clouds, so when the sun finally went down, the sky would be clear and full of stars—the benefit of living in a small town.

"Stop it; they're fine," Crispin said from the end of the picnic table we had set with a fancy tablecloth.

Eric had already made plans at a fancy restaurant outside of town when we told him our scheme, so it would just be us, Briar, and Maisie, which was fine because the picnic table wasn't all that big.

We lined the entire railing with those flickering fake candles Mom had used them for some event and then stowed them in the garage. We had real candles and two fancy cheeseboards decked out. Mom had also helped with this because when Crispin and I tried to do it on our own, it did not look elegant but like we were putting out some snacks for toddlers.

We had wine glasses filled with pomegranate and grape juice to mimic the look of wine.

"That girl has you all sorts of messed up."

"Agreed and not bothered," I said, sitting across from him only to bolt back up when I saw Briar's car pull up to the curb.

Mom and Dad were waiting in their car to take pictures. We tried to talk them out of it, but my mom wouldn't have it. Dad had gotten her a fancy camera for Christmas, and she was excited to use it.

I walked down the stairs and across the grass, nervously smoothing out my suit.

As I approached, she got out of her car, and I slowed to a stop before I even got to the curb.

I was frozen as she walked around the side of the car. She lifted the skirt of her dress to step up over the curb and then smiled at me as she stopped at the sidewalk doing Vanna White show-off hands as she spun around.

I was unwell.

I could not remember seeing a woman more beautiful in my natural life.

She walked toward me when I didn't say anything and tucked some hair behind her ear.

"Earth to Darcy, whaddya think?"

I walked forward and pulled her to me as she tripped on her shoes a bit and stumbled into me.

"I don't mean to be too ridiculous, Briar, but you look good enough to eat."

She colored a bit before recovering and pushed passed me. "Promises, promises."

We all ate after my mom took tons of pictures and took Maisie's and Briar's mom's emails to send them. Maisie FaceTimed her mom, who had gone with her father out of town. Briar's mom had to work, but she texted her some photos, including the table and candles setup.

"This is terrible," Maisie said more to Crispin than me. "Turns out you aren't completely incompetent."

"Well, you clean up nice, so I'm glad I didn't waste my time."

"Get a room," Briar interrupted then and rummaged around in her purse for a cylinder with a dial on it which she spun and removed the cap to reveal a needle.

"That's new?" I questioned.

"I didn't want to wear the pump with my dress." She shrugged; she pulled her sleeve up and injected herself in the bicep.

"Can't you do that, like not where we are eating?" Maisie asked, and I turned my head to say something to her but saw a half grin on Maisie's face.

"I'm not going to the bathroom for other people's comfort. Maisie knows you guys are vampires."

"And that is exactly why you should never play who is the bigger bitch game with Briar Grey," Maisie mumbled, looking down to a tomato she was rolling between her fingers.

Crispin and I looked at each other, and I blinked my surprise away. We thought there was a real possibility that Maisie knew as she belonged to the notorious Pope family, and obviously, Morgan knew.

"Are you a hunter?" Crispin asked the question we both wanted to know.

"Yes, but not like Morgan, not like...people that think you're evil or anything. My dad advocates for vampire rights and equality of life." Maisie looked down as if she were a little ashamed.

"Oh, that's nice. Your father advocates for basic human decency." Crispin scowled, and I winced a little.

On the other hand, Briar popped a cube of cheese into her mouth like it was popcorn, and she had front-row tickets to a good show.

"Some people would argue you aren't human at all," Maisie spat, before throwing me an apologetic look.

I knew whatever was happening was between her and Crispin. The barbs she threw out were not for me, so I reached out and grabbed one of those rock-hard breadsticks and crunched down on it.

"Seems like the people who take life into their own hands and judge who deserves to live and die based on a disease that one is born with are the inhuman ones." Crispin shot back

"Did you know that Crispin designed your corsage?" I interrupted.

"You ruin all my fun," Briar said under her breath, and the table went a little silent.

"Well, where is it then?" Maisie said, having understood I meant to change the subject.

I sprang up to get mine for Briar out of a cooler with ice, and Crispin rolled his eyes and made a great show of taking his time.

I grabbed mine and walked over to Briar. I was too proud of it for not having done much.

I sat next to her and slipped it over her fingers and onto her wrist. The colors were stark against her pale skin. I turned her wrist around and leaned down to kiss the pulse point on the edge of her palm.

Her blood sang to me under the thick layers of skin. I remembered what one drop of it had tasted like, and my eyelids fluttered closed as I imagined the warm liquid flowing over my tongue. The fantasy was only fueled by whatever maddening scent she wore on special occasions, and the fresh coconut fragrance muddled my thoughts.

I pulled away, but she caught my wrist and spun the friendship bracelet she had made me around once.

"You're wearing this to prom?"

"I don't take it off."

"Freak."

"That ankle pic got me all bothered."

She turned away so I wouldn't see her blush. It was one of my favorite things that she did.

"It's beautiful, Crispin." I heard Maisie say as she gave a half smile to her corsage.

"Don't sound so surprised, Pope," he replied.

"Don't ruin this, you asshole; just shut up." I rolled my eyes, picked up a black olive, and threw it at Crispin's head.

"She fucking started it," he said, jabbing a thumb in her direction in a juvenile display of defiance.

Crispin, who kept me calm and levelheaded when I started to get too much anxiety, was brought down by an eighteen-year-old girl in a sparkly pink dress.

He grumbled something under his breath, and Maisie shot him a look of victory.

"Whaddya say, guys? Should we head that way? They need me there fifteen minutes early to ensure I fit into my crown," I joked, but only Maisie smiled.

"If we must," Briar said as I stood up and offered her my elbow.

Chapter Thirty

Briar

"Punch?" Darcy asked me where I stood, frozen at the edge of the chaos that was Ironside's prom.

"Is there even punch here?" I said, looking up at his ever-present smile.

"No, but I've always seen it in movies, and I wanted to say it."

"You sure are a strange bird."

"You know you love me." He wove his fingers into mine, and my heart beat faster. Not out of affection but fear as his words scraped against something I didn't want to think about.

I was on edge. I felt one of my bad moods like a fog over a great expanse of water. It threatened to overtake me. I could dispel it if I wanted to, but I wasn't sure I didn't want to ruin this.

All I could think about driving my car over here was that I had more fun at dinner than I wanted to. I liked the people I was with more than I ever planned. I had reached out for Darcy's hand more than once subconsciously. Damn my traitor heart.

I had let myself fall in love with him, which was evident to me now, and I was on edge with every word he spoke and brush of his hand.

One more month of school left, but our deal no longer stood now: I told him I would be his girlfriend. This meant I would have to deal with our relationship when I started working and he started attending school. Sure, he would still be local, and so would I, but I was scared shitless of what that meant.

High school relationships were fun, flirty things that hardly amounted to anything. After graduation, it was an adult relationship, and I was in love with the dude. A sweet basketball-playing boy who made me want to fall into his warm sunshine.

Was I becoming warm sunshine?

I was vile and explosive on purpose. I didn't want to be soft; I wanted to be volatile. It protected me. It would protect me if he decided I wasn't worth the trouble. He might be moon-ey-eyed now, but the novelty of my personality would wear off soon, and he would leave just like almost everyone else.

"You, okay?" Darcy asked, furrowing a little as my insides turned into panic soup.

I opened my mouth to say something. What? I didn't know. Was I going to assure him I was okay or tell him I wasn't?

"Junior and Senior class, please welcome your prom king and queen to the Stage. Darcy Booker and Kia Kumari, please make your way up to the stage." An adult's voice rang out over the crowd of students who had just gotten done dancing to a remix of baby shark.

"Be right back?" he questioned, leaning in to press a soft kiss to my cheek.

I nodded, ushering him forward, knowing I would bolt as soon as possible. He jogged to the stage and offered Kia his arm, and they walked up the stairs together.

Jealousy and unsettling questions coursed through my brain. It crippled me as I chastised myself. Envy piled on top of the other emotions I was experiencing, and I realized just how stupid I was. I had let myself become a lovesick doe-eyed idiot for Darcy. So much so that his offering his arm to another girl with a silly school title next to him had me worked up.

The fact that I was upset made me the most upset as the raincloud of my temperament settled over me. I stared despondently as Kia was handed flowers, the class cheered for her, and a sparkly tiara was placed on her head.

Stupid fucking sparkly ass tiara on her pretty stupid face. With her silly kind smile as she beamed out over the crowd.

Darcy bent a little to accept the gold crown on his head and smiled at everyone as they announced them. I couldn't hear anything. I could see only how they matched. Her blue dress swished as she turned, and they smiled at each other with their happiness radiating out over the kids, who soaked it up like dry dirt.

And maybe that was what bothered me the most. I knew Darcy belonged with someone like that, and I would never be that. I could never be that. Even if I became a little less... moody and hormonal, I could never be the girl that would smile out at life with him. I would always be me. I would never be sunshine, and I didn't want to care this much when he realized I wouldn't change.

I backed up toward the exit as the crowd of teenagers cheered again, and a bass-filled song started to play in the gymnasium decorated with golden sparkles and balloons. I reached the double doors as tears threatened. No one noticed me, and I could slip out without much fuss. But as I opened the door to leave, I made the mistake of looking up at the stage one last time. My heart slammed into my throat when I saw Darcy staring at me with narrowed eyes. He was locked onto me, and I sprinted (well, walked very fast, given my dress and shoe situation) into the hallway and to the exit.

I took the shoes off on the way so I could run—all the way to my car. I slowed when I was almost there and nearly groaned in frustration as I saw my boyfriend leaning against my driver's side door. His ridiculous gold crown was still sitting atop his head.

How the fuck did he get here before me?

"Where you goin'?" he accused, and I wasn't sure, but I thought I heard the distinct influx of irritation.

"I'm not feeling great; I'm going home."

"Without saying anything? You weren't going to tell me?" Not irritation; I had hurt his feelings. His tone told me everything I needed to know.

Put your heart away, you moron.

"I don't have to tell you where I'm going. You aren't my babysitter." I seethed, my anger an easy reach for me.

His brows furrowed, and a wave of guilt crashed over me as I saw the words hit their mark.

"What's wrong with you?" His tone was sharp, his hurt turning into anger.

"Fuck off, Darcy; I'm going home." I stepped forward, but he didn't move.

"Get off my car."

"No, I don't think I will."

It was frightening to see no humor or softness in his features.

"You're going to ruin this, and it's going great. We had fun at dinner, and you look incredible, and I was going to dance with you." He said it like a matter-of-fact thing.

"I don't want to dance. I don't want to play happy teenage girlfriend with you anymore. I don't want to be the picture of high school enjoyment. It's not me. It's you."

"What are you talking about? It isn't a show. I'm not showing you off. I don't want to be with you here to fulfill some high school fantasy."

"Good because I am not the fantasy type." I reached for my door handle, and he grabbed my arm. I stared up at him, shocked.

"Listen, Briar; you need to get your shit together, okay. You think you're tougher and cooler than everyone else. Maybe you are a little bit, but everyone has trauma. Your hard life doesn't make you any better than everyone else."

It was unapologetic, and I pulled my arm back from him and recoiled a little.

"You want to run away from this? Fine. You want to go back moping around the halls every day until graduation? Go ahead." He pushed off the car, the anger still radiating off him.

"I will," I defied as he took a few steps away from my car.

"You act like this big jerk of Ironside, but you're fucking scared. You are as scared as every other teenager that you think you're better than. The only difference between you and others is that you think you're entitled to treat people like shit whenever you want."

"I don't give a shit what you think of me." That was a lie. I heard it in the shakiness of my voice as tears threatened again.

"I can't believe I'm in love with the most selfish woman in this town." He shook his head, taking another step away.

I froze with my hand on the handle of my car. My stomach bottomed out, and my eyes snapped over to him, where he seemed unfazed by the admission.

"What?" I questioned, looking up at him as every thought flooded from me but the words he had just spoken.

"You. Are. Selfish." He punctuated every word, and I nearly smiled.

It was the friendly people you had to watch out for. You didn't want to piss off a nice person. Because the thing was, their threshold for your bullshit was so much higher. When you finally cracked their patience, it was so much worse.

"No before that?" My voice was soft, and his anger flickered to confusion, his features grappling with the question before realizing its meaning.

"Oh," he said, a little dazed, reaching up to rub the back of his neck.

Chapter Thirty-One

Darcy

"Oh?" she asked after a long silence between us. The only thing to be heard was the loud, raucous music being played inside the gym, and even that was muted as if it was leaving me alone to come back from saying I loved Briar.

What kind of idiot told his girlfriend he loved her for the first time while arguing? Followed 'I'm in love ' up with 'by the way, you're selfish, so peace out'. I did. Now, I was frozen, staring at her with a violent blush across my face. My heart rate was so elevated that I felt my fangs drop down.

"That's not exactly how I meant to tell you that," I admitted as she stood nearly slack-jawed by her car.

"How had you meant to?"

"How had I meant to what?"

I couldn't think about how mad I had been.

And I had been mad. Mad at her for taking off, trying to leave, and then throwing words at me like it was my fault she was constantly in a bad mood. Angry at myself for accepting prom king. Mad that she was right, and I expected her to be...not like me but the rest of us. I was angry that I had hoped she would try and fit in.

"I know..." I started, unsure of what to say now. I had fully intended to leave her out here, but my accidental revelation had shifted the tone. So I walked back to her a few steps. "I know your dad is kinda shitty. Hell, I met him, and he seemed like a complete tool. And Morgan, don't even get me started on Morgan."

"What do they have to do with anything?" Her words were harsh but not meant to cut me, she had softened a bit, and I took more steps toward her.

"I just mean, I get that you haven't had great men experiences."

"Men experiences?" she questioned, and I groaned, running my hand over my face. Why was I such an idiot? But when I looked back at her, she had a ghost of a smile on her face, and her eyebrow was raised.

"You're making fun of me." I breathed out.

"It's kind of hard not to you're being a moron."

I walked until I was in front of her, and she turned, looked up at me and leaned back against her door.

"You hurt my feelings by leaving the dance without saying anything. And I'm sorry if it's not very masculine or whatever to say. You hurt my feelings...."

"I'm sorry I hurt your feelings. I meant to." She reached out and laced her fingers in mine, turning her face down and away from me. "But I'm still sorry."

"Why are you trying to hurt my feelings, girl? Can't you see I'm a sensitive, delicate man?" I put my fingers under her chin to force her to look at me.

"I didn't mean to...like you as much as I like you. And I'm scared."

"All right. I can work with that. We can chill out and dial it back if you need...."

"I love you...I mean, I love you too...back."

My stomach bottomed out as I stared down at her. Some part of me wondered if anyone would ever say that to me. My parents loved me, of course, and Crispin, and I assumed if I married another vampire who wasn't... disgusted by who I was but never a human girl. It seemed so far out of the realm of possibility.

I had been taught that no one would understand. That humans wouldn't get it. But Briar had never once made me feel like I was any less of something because of my vampirism.

She stared up at me with glittery eyes and hesitation in her gaze. Her mouth was painted a deep purple, now begging me to kiss her.

"Your fangs are out," she said, reaching up to touch my lip below where the sharp part of my lateral canine poked out.

I pulled back a little, covering my mouth with my hand. I was overwhelmed by emotion, and warm, soft happiness was pulsing through me. My fangs had never come out because I was happy before. Maybe it was because I was fighting off the thoughts of what it would be like to push Briar up against her car and kiss her until she was breathless.

She took my hand away from my mouth. "It doesn't bother me. They're kinda cute."

It was the last straw on my fragile teenage self-control as I pushed myself into her frame and cupped one of her cheeks in my hands, pressing a kiss to her mouth.

It wasn't a soft or gentle kiss, and I wasn't as patient as I had been before. I made sure my fangs didn't puncture her. My mouth crashed into her. She sighed into my me and pulled me closer by the waist of my slacks. Her fingers lingered there, and I savored the feel of her pressed against me.

With my hand on her neck, I pushed her head to the side as I kissed down the soft column of her throat.

"When you inevitably break up with me because I'm too golden retriever for your gothic ass, I need you to tell me what perfume you wear." I kissed between words becoming dizzy with the small sounds she made when I kissed a sensitive spot.

"Shut up; you're always talking." She reached up and slipped my unbuttoned jacket over my shoulders.

We were separated for a moment and then came back together. I peppered her face with kisses, telling her I loved her between every one, kissing her against her smile. I didn't even care if I sounded like an idiot. I was still living off the high of her telling me she loved me.

We broke apart to the sound of a loud screeching alarm from the school. We both turned, trying to sort out what was going on.

"Fire alarm," Briar said first as the short, loud bursts were interrupted by screaming kids pouring out of the gymnasium. We walked toward them as teachers yelled instructions that no one was paying attention to. Most kids were still laughing, only upset about the fact they got a little wet. As we passed most of them, I heard everyone planning to move the party somewhere else.

I held Briar's hand as we went against the current of kids. I smelled the air, not detecting any trace of smoke. Briar's eyes shot around and landed on Trudy and Eric as she waved them over. They came to us looking nearly as confused as we were, only they were wet.

"Crispin? Maisie?" Briar asked, but Trudy and Eric shook their heads.

My eyes surveyed the crowd, and I could see almost everything.

"Crispin," I hollered as I saw him looking around wildly. He located me and came over, looking panicked.

"What is it?" I asked him, setting my hands on his shoulder.

"I can't find Maisie." The hard edge of anxiety layered his words, and I saw him trying to control his breathing.

"What do you mean?"

"I mean, she went outside to smoke and never came back, and then the alarm went off, and I can't find her."

"Sometimes she smokes by the soccer field in the back; Erik and I will check." Trudy volunteered, and they took off in that direction.

"There is no fire," Crispin said to me low, and his eyes flashed red for the briefest moment. "So, who pulled the fire alarm."

He was panicking, making connections where there might be none. His hair clung to his face. He scanned the crowd of kids repeatedly, looking for her.

"Probably some stupid senior prank," Briar said, and I was surprised at how soothing her tone was. She could see he was on edge.

"Yeah, that's probably it," I said, nodding to him. "But let's go inside and check. All the teachers will be out here trying to control the chaos. We can slip in."

"The noise, I can handle it. I don't want you guys to have to go in." Crispin almost cringed at his own idea.

The alarm was loud, and something loud to humans was deafening to us. Disorienting even.

"With three of us, it won't take long," I said, releasing him and setting my sites on the school as I heard firetrucks in the distance.

"And I'm not standing out here like an idiot while everyone else is looking for her, so let's stop standing around," Briar said, walking toward the school's entrance.

Chapter Thirty-Two

Briar

The sound was awful. It scraped my nerves as we walked into the school. Crispin and Darcy were freaking out, their eyelids opening and closing as if they could blink the sound away. Their fangs were out and bared, and their eyes glowed red; seeming almost illuminated in the dark hallways of the school.

Maisie was probably outside. Hopefully, Trudy and Eric had found her, but Crispin's panicked face twisted my insides. He didn't seem prone to violent displays of worry, so we walked down the darkened main hallway.

It was a little spooky at night, with no one else around and the fire alarm screeching its warning down the bare halls. Not to mention the two vampires walking next to me with double fangs bared, touching their heads every so often. I should have just come to look. But they could smell things and hear things I couldn't. So I followed them at a crawling pace as they kept taking breaks.

Suddenly the screeching stopped. The alarms turned off, and both the boys let out a groan of relief.

"There's no fucking fire," Crispin said with almost a growl. "When I find the damn person who pulled that alarm, I'm going to rip their throat out and lap their fresh blood off the floor."

"He's being dramatic." Darcy assured me, giving Crispin a cautionary look.

"And if I find out Maisie was just finding a new place to smoke her damned cigarettes, I'm going to kill her too."

"Nobody is going to kill anyone," Darcy said, holding his hands out. "Can you stop saying stuff like that in front of my girlfriend?"

"Am I bothering you, Briar?" Crispin asked, turning to me.

"Nope. If we find the person, who did it, I'll hold the bastard down while you drain him dry." I said to lighten the mood and a little to get a reaction from Darcy.

That is precisely what I got as he looked at me wide-eyed. Crispin threw his head back and the hallways reverberated with his laughter.

"Yeah, this is not my favorite," Darcy said, and I slipped my hand into his, which Crispin tracked with his eyes and gave Darcy a smug smile.

"Wait," Darcy said, and we all went quiet.

They both could hear something though I couldn't.

"What is it?" I asked.

"Maisie, she's yelling," Crispin growled and took off down the hall at a pace I would never be able to keep.

Inhumane speed.

"Go," I said to Darcy, shooing him with my hands. "I'll just slow you down. I'll be right behind you."

He nodded and bolted the same way Crispin disappeared before I could ask which way to go. I didn't even bother to run. What use would I be? Also, I didn't even know in which direction to run. I stopped dead, wondering if I would be better off going back outside and waiting for them.

"Briar!" Someone called behind me, and I turned to roll my eyes as Morgan jogged down the hall toward me.

"Go away, for the love of everything good in this world, read the room." I rolled my eyes and turned back around.

"I was just checking to see that you were okay; I saw you come in here with the Bookers."

"Oh yes, and you thought something terrible was going to happen to me. I like them, Morgan, despite your threats and warnings,"

"Briar, come with me, just out front, please. Please, let's wait for them out there." His voice was strained. Something was wrong, and as I looked back at him, I began to feel uneasy. A cold chill ripped through me as I saw the desperate expression on his face.

"Do you have something to do with this? With the fire alarm?" I accused him.

"Briar, listen, you don't understand. There are things I can't tell you. Things you don't know. If you knew and understood what they mean, you wouldn't be so eager to follow the Booker Brothers." His eyes shifted to the shadows of the hallway behind him, and he rubbed his arms nervously.

"I know things," I said, which I felt was both ambiguous enough that it wasn't a confirmation, but helped my point still the same. "I'd rather follow them than follow you, and you better hope that I don't tell Crispin you pulled the alarm because he is looking for someone to beat up." I turned back, taking a confident step away form from him.

"Briar," he pleaded with me, and the spark of irritation I had felt blossomed into anger.

"Listen, fuckface."

Before I could finish, I was grabbed from behind. A hand wrapped around my mouth, and I let out a scream of fear against their palm before biting down hard. There was a grunt of pain, but the person didn't move their hand from my mouth even as I tasted the blood on my lips.

I kicked and tried to fall to the floor, but the arms pulled me against them.

I could not remember one single self-defense lesson that had been taught to me. I was tugged around and dragged toward a classroom door.

Morgan came into view, and I was surprised that it wasn't him who was holding me. His eyes offered me an apology as he held up a syringe full of something and took a step toward me.

My eyes were wide, my heartbeat erratic. I bucked and kicked against my captor, who held me with stone-like strength. I used my eyes to shoot daggers at Morgan, and an expression I hoped said, 'don't you fucking do it'.

"Come on, pansy boy, stick her. I can't hold her like this forever; she's strong for a girl." It was a deep voice that spoke above me, sounding sort of like Morgan but older and meaner.

"Sorry, Briar," Morgan stepped forward, and I screamed against the person's palm and tried to back away. My heartbeat pulsed in my ears, and I felt adrenaline course through me, but nothing was enough.

I pushed and kicked and screamed but the needle bit into my neck anyway.

After a few seconds of wondering if I was going to die, there was nothing but a sleepy blackness that I tumbled into.

Chapter Thirty-Three

Darcy

The door had been jammed with one of the heavy chairs from a classroom, and Maisie banged around inside, yelling all sorts of swear words that would make a sailor blush. Hell, I was blushing. She flew out of the maintenance closet in attack position and screamed as she threw herself at Crispin, who had opened the door.

We should have announced ourselves as she was now on top of him with her hands around his throat.

"You've crunched something in me that was not meant to be crunched." He moaned, blinking up at her.

"You'll live." She climbed off him as gracefully as one could. "You guys are okay?"

She seemed concerned, confused even. She tried to straighten her dress, stuffing her hands down the front of her top unceremoniously to adjust her boobs as I awkwardly looked up at the ceiling.

"Why wouldn't we be?" Crispin groaned as he got up, resting his hands on his knees for a moment.

I looked back as Maisie ripped the tulle off from around her shoulders in irritation and threw the cotton candy-like mess on the ground in anger.

"My stupid cousins locked me in there, calling me a vampire-loving whore and all kinds of other things, saying that's what I got for taking sides with The Booker Brothers. I just assumed they were here to try something."

"We didn't even see Morgan. Was he even at Prom?"

"Yeah, he was, and when I was done smoking, I came inside to use the restroom, and he and my older cousin, Adam. Who, believe it or not, is worse than Morgan..." she trailed off.

"Worse in what way?" I asked.

"More devout to the old ways. Hunters killing vampires for no reason or cause. Just that he thinks we were created to cleanse the world."

"He must be fun at parties," Crispin commented. "Are you okay? Did they hurt you?"

"My pride mostly. I want to say that I could kick their asses, but they picked me up and threw me in that closet like I weighed nothing."

"They pulled the fire alarm?" I looked at the broken fire alarm case across the hall from us.

"Must have; it started a little after I was in the closet."

"Well, we haven't seen them, so whatever the asswipes were trying to do, they seem to be failing. Other than throwing you in the closet and ruining prom."

"Let's go get Briar. Trudy and Erik went to look for you on the soccer field."

We walked down the halls, and now that the alarms weren't blaring, I noticed a lot more. The floors were wet, and our shoes squeaked against them. Maisie stopped at one point to take off her heels.

Briar wasn't in the hallway where I had left her, and I felt a tightness squeeze my chest as I wondered if she had left. Maybe she had just waited for us to find Maisie and had left after all. After everything, after I told her I loved her and... no. I shook off the insecure part of me that had started speaking. Briar said she loved me.

We might have just had our first fight or disagreement, but she said she loved me and wouldn't leave now. I didn't think.

We went out the doors we had entered, and the front of the school was nearly empty except for teachers and firefighters. It was dark, and the bright ugly school lights illuminated everything in a sickly green glow.

"Kids, what the hell are you doing?" A firefighter yelled as the door slammed behind us. They shined flashlights into our eyes, and I instinctively covered my face with my hand, ensuring my fangs weren't out.

"We haven't cleared that building!"

"Maisie, Darcy, Crispin!" Mrs. Sheridan shooed us over as we walked to her.

"What were you all doing in the school? The dance was in the gym," she chastised.

We all stayed silent, not knowing what to say to explain ourselves, and she sighed, pinching the bridge of her nose.

"I don't even want to know." She held up a hand. "We've sent all the other students home. I'm sorry about your prom."

"It's okay, Mrs. S; have you seen Briar?" I asked.

"Briar? No? I've been stationed out here almost the whole time; I haven't seen her."

I frowned, a trepidatious feeling settling into the pit of my stomach.

"Go home, don't cause trouble, and don't make me regret not getting you in trouble for being in the school when you weren't supposed to be."

"Thanks, Mrs. Sheridan," Crispin said in his best flirty tone.

"Save it, Crispin. I would have written you up if you hadn't been with Miss Pope and your brother. Their good character has given you a free pass."

"That's cold." He passed her, but she smiled and shook her head, turning her back to us as we walked away.

"Mais!" Trudy called from across the parking lot, standing by Erik's car.

"You okay? We were starting to worry," Erik said, pulling Maisie in for a hug before Trudy got to her.

"Yeah, totally fine. I went inside the school to pee, then the alarms went off, and I was freaked out."

The inflection of her voice never changed. The lie was seamless. My grandpa on my father's side used to tell me to watch out for a good liar, and my grandma would battle his pessimism and say, "everyone tells their first lie for a reason." I wondered what Maisie's first lie had been.

"Have you guys seen Briar?" I asked.

"Nope, her car is still here, in any case. That must mean she's here, right?"

"I guess," I shrugged, looking around. Where the hell would she have gone?

"You guys wanna come over and watch a movie? I know it's not prom, but I have popcorn and a bunch of snacks my stoner brother buys for himself," Erik asked.

"Sounds fun," Crispin said distantly. "We gotta call our mom, but we'll text you."

"Cool," Erik nodded.

"I better get home, but thanks, raincheck." Maisie gave Trudy one last hug before she got into Erik's car, and they pulled away.

We waved in the dark parking lot, and I glanced at Briar's car. I walked over slowly, feeling the anxiety in me build as I realized there was glass littered by her passenger side door.

"Crispin," I called in a warning voice, and he was by my side in an instant.

Glass crunched under my feet as I peered inside the broken window. Her phone was gone; she told me she had left it on her seat, but the zipper pouch with insulin was still in there.

Crispin walked around to the front of her car, and I looked up as I heard the crinkle of a piece of paper.

"Why did the vampire break up with his girlfriend?" He read off the notebook paper shoved under one of her windshield wipers.

"She wasn't his type," Maisie answered, looking over the car's damage.

A bad joke we had all heard before, but now it was threatening.

I snatched the paper out of Crispin's hand, eyes scanning the rest of the note. My heart thundered in my chest, and I felt dizzy, unable to hear Crispin as he tried to say something to me.

"One four one three Whipper Downs road, come alone, or you won't have a girlfriend when you come through the door."

Chapter Thirty-Four

Briar

I shook my hands against the bindings around the back of the chair. The black cord bit into my wrists and was tied tight enough so that I couldn't get out, but it only hurt if I tried to wiggle my hands too much. I had been sitting in front of a television with my ankles tied to the same chair. I thought Morgan was in the bathroom clearing up the bloody nose I had given him by smacking my head into it while he was tying my arms.

It had taken both for my legs, one to hold me down while the other tied.

Adam was Morgan's older brother, whom I had only met once in passing when we were dating. I only really remembered Adam because he had made some off-color joke about my weight. One of those things that was supposed to sound like a compliment, but I knew he was a fat-phobic jackass. It did not surprise me that he also hated vampires on principle.

He referred to Darcy and Crispin as either "the bloodsucker brothers" or "the leeches," only Morgan used their names.

Adam had gone to get something to eat after I head-butted Morgan. He had come at me like he was going to throttle me and Morgan yelled at him to get gone.

I tried my best to be unbothered, but Adam was a psycho. You could see in his eyes that he didn't give two shits if I got hurt in the process of whatever their plan was.

I told myself to breathe. That it was going to be okay, Darcy and Crispin would go to the police, and they would come and get me. Or the Booker brothers would show up on their own, and there would be a hunter/vampire showdown before my eyes.

My phone screeched on the kitchen counter where it was sitting. One of them had broken into my car to get it. Unfortunately, they had not grabbed my insulin bag, and I couldn't check my sugar.

It was probably low based on the mild shake, the increased heart rate, and my lack of ability to hold a good train of thought.

I waited a few more minutes to make sure it wasn't just general anxiety, but as it dropped lower and lower, I felt myself fading.

I considered just dying for a moment out of spite. Get these assholes on manslaughter as well as kidnapping. Alas, I had too much to live for.

"Hey, jackass!" I called as my phone screeched again.

I heard his footfall through the empty house they had brought me to. Who knows where, but aside from my chair and the television, there wasn't much else. A kitchen table with four diner-like red faux leather chairs. A refrigerator that I could see. There might have been beds in the bedrooms, but I couldn't see beyond the bare living room I was in and an open doorway to the kitchen.

"Why is your phone making that noise?" he asked, tapping the screen.

"Open it up. The password is three two seven two nine. Click on the notification that is at the top about my glucose level."

He did as I asked, tapping away and staring at the screen.

"What does it say?"

"Forty-one."

Not good.

"Is the arrow next to it in the middle kinda down or straight down?" I asked, hating that I had to rely on him to answer the questions.

"Straight down"

Super not good.

"You better find me some sugar to eat unless you want me to die tied to this chair. Then you can be tried for murder. You're eighteen, aren't you? How does life in prison sound?"

"Hold on." He didn't look overly concerned as he stepped out of view, and I heard cupboards opening and closing.

"Any day now, genius, it's only getting lower." I had broken out into a cold sweat. I felt heavy and useless. If I wanted to escape right now, I couldn't.

"What about this?" He came into view, holding up a grape Kool-Aid packet.

"Would be great if you didn't have to add sugar to that to make it sweet."

"I have sugar."

"Well, mix some up then!" It was a yell, a scream that echoed through the empty house, but I was fading, and if Morgan killed me over not knowing he needed to put sugar in Kool-Aid, I would haunt him when I died.

He took his sweet time as the seconds of my life ticked by. He came into view with a tall pink plastic cup and stepped over to me.

I didn't have time to think of how much I hated him putting the cup to my lips. I could only drink the artificial grape beverage as fast as I could. It was warm, and I drank half of it before he pulled it away.

"More?"

"Hold on a minute."

I took long deep breaths, my mind telling my body it wasn't dying; to hold on a minute till the sugar hit my bloodstream.

"B?" he asked, using a nickname he had used when we were dating. I opened my eyes to give him a dark look.

"More," I demanded, and he lifted the cup to my lips again for me to drink.

"You can't tell me you don't enjoy this a little," he said, smiling down at me.

I jerked my whole body back, and the chair went with me.

I spit the entire mouthful of warm syrupy liquid in his face as he sputtered and stumbled back.

"I am not enjoying it. First, I don't like you, and second, you kidnapped me. So even if I did like you, any amount before that has been completely wiped away."

"You still wanted me when I broke up with you. You would give me puppy dog eyes in the hall."

My anger flared, but not at Morgan. I had moped around school after our breakup. I was ashamed that he was able to tell. That meant everyone knew, and a hot wave of embarrassment coursed through me.

"Not anymore; I don't think of you at all."

I met his eyes as he wiped his face on his sleeve. The asshole had the audacity to look wounded.

"Because of the basketball-playing moron?" His voice was soft and hesitant, and I gave him a disgusted look as I tried to sort out the confusion his reaction elicited.

"Yes, because of Darcy."

"So that's what you wanted? Someone to turn you into a jock girlfriend. Look at you, Briar, going to prom? Basketball games? Hanging out with my cousin, Maisie "the Princess" Pope. Dating a dork that looks after you with moon eyes."

I didn't know what to say. Some of what Morgan said cut into me and the insecurity I felt leaving prom.

"Darcy isn't trying to change me into anything."

"Well, whether he is or isn't, you have. This isn't you, Briar."

"You lost the right to comment on my behavior when you broke up with me because I wouldn't sleep with you."

"That's not why I broke up with you!" he yelled at me and looked as young as he was for a moment. Beyond the tattoos and the black clothes. "I didn't want you involved in this." He gestured around like it explained everything. "Something your boyfriend doesn't seem to care about, and now look at you."

"Oh yes, it's Darcy's fault you kidnapped me."

"He should know better than to get involved with a human with what he is. If he cared about you, he would leave you alone."

"He cared about me enough to let me make my own choices."

We glared at each other from across the room for a long time before he stomped off to the kitchen.

"I need my insulin!" I yelled after him. "You grabbed my phone but left my insulin in my car!"

"Don't you wear a pump?" he asked.

"In this dress? No, I don't."

"I'll go grab it when Adam comes back."

"You're going to leave me with him?"

"He won't hurt you." He came into view and leaned against the open doorway.

"He looked like he was going to."

"Don't talk back to him. He's just a hothead. If you stay quiet, he'll leave you alone."

"Know that from experience?" I meant to ask as an insult, but my tone was more concerned as his eyes gave me the answer I needed.

"Shut the fuck up, Briar. I'm going into the other room until Adam comes back. Then I'll get your damn insulin. Fucking pain in my ass."

I tried not to feel sorry for him as he left my sight, and I heard the springs of an old mattress creak and another television turn on. I didn't want to have any sympathy for him. He didn't deserve it.

I closed my eyes and leaned back, hoping Darcy would hurry up and rescue me.

I knew this one thing for sure.

He was just the sort of gentleman to save a girl who tried to ghost him at prom. He would come.

Chapter Thirty-Five

Darcy

I paced my room with Crispin and Maisie sitting on my bed. We had to be quiet because my parents were sleeping downstairs.

"We can't get the police involved," Maisie stated again, and Crispin rolled his eyes at her.

"We know the rules, Maisie," Crispin said. "We know it goes against the treaty to call human cops on a vampire-hunter matter."

Somewhere in this house that Adam and Morgan were trying to lure us to, Briar was sitting. The night wore on, and she was without her insulin, and we were sitting here like idiots deciding what to do. I was going out of my mind with worry and panic. I wasn't the violent type, but when I got my hands on Morgan, I was going to wrap my fingers around his throat and squeeze until he could no longer breathe. I'd let up when he turned purple. The brain damage would be minimal.

"It's my fault she's in this situation. This is exactly why Mom and Dad don't want us to date in high school. She's in danger, and for what? Because some teenage boy is jealous, or his dad and older brother think all vampires are demons from hell? I did this to her. She wouldn't have even been on their radar."

"Whether that is true or not, it doesn't help her now," Maisie said. "And if it weren't her, it would have been someone else. At least she's tough. I hope she kicked the shit out of them a little."

That thought made me smile a bit. If Briar had been able to fight, she would have.

"They won't kill her, and I don't think they'll hurt her either. Morgan won't, at least. I know it's hard to imagine, but I think he really...loved Briar when they dated. Plus, she's a human. They only kill vampires."

Jealousy panged through me as my mind pulled up mental images of Morgan's arms wrapped around Briar. I shoved it aside because it wasn't the time or place for teenage rivalry.

"Do you think about what you say before you say it?" Crispin asked, his tone irritated.

"I was just trying to say...."

"Maybe don't try to say next time," he snapped.

"A lot of good you are doing sitting there like the stone statue of David."

"Guys!" I nearly shouted, and they both jumped a little. "Can you just not for one moment? We have bigger things to deal with."

I heard two mumbled apologies as I rubbed my thumb along the opposite palm and stared at the ceiling.

"We can't go in the house. They're counting on us to go in the house and break the treaty. Then they have full right to kill us with no repercussions. Mom and Dad won't be able to do anything."

"But I can invite you into the house," Maisie said thoughtfully.

"What?" I stopped pacing to look at her.

"They are at a family house, like a safe house. Their dad and my dad's names are on the deed, so technically, I can invite you in."

"What are we supposed to do? Go in guns blazing? Kick down the doors and get into an all-out war with your cousins?" My voice frayed, the thread unraveling me, and now Crispin and Masie could see it too.

Maisie looked startled, which was fair. In most situations, I tried my hardest to keep a calm and level head. I tried to be the light when things got negative, but I was struggling now. It seemed like our only two options were to attempt a teenage rescue and maybe get shot up by some crazy purist slayers, or tell my parents and wait two business days for OOVA to come down here and intervene.

I would have had no problem choosing option two, but I didn't know how long Briar could go without her medicine. My parents would no doubt make the better, more rational choice, but what if her health took a terrible turn for the worse in that time? Her idiot of an ex certainly didn't care. He hadn't even remembered to grab her supplies. That thought drove my mind to become dark and monstrous.

The devil within me reveled in the thought of ripping his throat open for hurting her. That he would dare touch her with mal intent. I took a deep breath and banished the darkness with a wipe of the slate. I wouldn't feed that thought process. Morgan was young and a product of his environment. While I was angry at him for involving Briar, I knew his family had raised him to be like that.

If I had been raised by anyone else, I might have become the monster he feared I was. No, Morgan wasn't the villain and did not deserve to bleed out on the floor. However, if I got to hit him just once in the face...surely that was deserved?

"You won't get in trouble with your family for helping us?" I asked Maisie, formulating a plan in my head that I knew would probably backfire.

"Maybe." She shrugged. "I'm not that worried about it. Briar is my friend, and so are you guys. I'll do whatever I can."

For once, Crispin wasn't looking at Maisie like he was trying to figure out his next well-placed insult to hurl at her. He nodded her way in appreciation.

"OOVA is coming tomorrow, which means we will have to do it before they come and be back in time."

"Early then?" Maisie asked, and I nodded.

"Let's meet at the gas station at the edge of town at five thirty," I said. "We try to do this as peacefully as possible. No one gets hurt."

"What about Morgan?" Crispin asked.

"Not even Morgan." I bit back my anger, trying to be as understanding as possible.

"Not even a little bit?" Crispin asked. "Bones heal."

"Briar is without her medicine. So the most important thing is getting her to her supplies and making sure she doesn't need to go to the hospital. I don't want this to escalate. I prefer that Mom and Dad didn't know until after."

I'd tell them about everything, all of it; after she was safe.

"Dad will kill us," Crispin said, looking off in the distance like he was already picturing the blimp-sized lecture our father would dole out when I told him everything that had been happening.

But I also trusted my dad. I knew that if I ever got drunk at a party or was in a situation I wasn't supposed to be in but felt unsafe, I could call him, and he would come to get me. No questions asked. A light lecture? Sure, that's what dads were for. But my dad loved and trusted us. I hadn't felt right about keeping things from him and Mom for the past couple of weeks.

"One early morning rescue, one routine OOVA visit, and then the scolding of a lifetime."

"Let's fucking do it." Crispin nodded at me.

Chapter Thirty-Six

Briar

I'd slept in the chair they had me tied up in.

Chivalry was dead in this household. I woke up in the dark, unsure of what time it was. I was sure, however, that my neck was permanently damaged from sleeping with my head lulled forward.

Hushed voices in the kitchen had woken me. They were becoming less quiet as what they were saying took on the tone of an argument.

"I have to go get her insulin," Morgan said, irritated. "She could die, and then what? We don't kill humans."

"You sure your feelings aren't clouding your judgment on this, boy?" A gruff voice asked. Deeper than Adam's. "You still in love with her? Is that why you are acting like this?"

"The deal was to use Briar as bait to get Crispin and Darcy here. She was never supposed to be in danger. We've put her in danger now, and I'm not going to let her go into a coma, or whatever will happen to her if she doesn't have her medicine." Morgan's tone was hard as steel and didn't seem like it left much room for argument.

"Fine, but you go get it and come right back. There is no telling when they will be here."

"Don't touch her, Adam; I swear if you so much as raise a hand to her."

"I won't touch your pretty little girlfriend, Morgan. Get the fuck out already," Adam snapped at him, making me flinch at the words, even in the dark.

I heard shuffling and a door opening and closing. It was still dark outside, so I couldn't see much. I realized I had no idea what time it was, but I guessed early morning.

"Hey, assholes!" I yelled into the dark, and all movement stopped, as the house went silent. "I have to pee. You want to clean it off the floor, or will you let me use the damn bathroom?"

Finally, after several beats of silence, there was movement. Heavy footfall came toward me as my eyes adjusted to the dim lighting. A figure stopped in the doorway of the room I was in. Tall and somewhat menacing; not Adam or Morgan.

He got closer, and I could finally make his features as he stood before me.

"Hey, Mr. Pope, long time no see."

Morgan's dad was a tall man with the same dark hair as his son, only peppered with grey and tied back behind his head. His frown was set deep into the wrinkles he had earned from making the same face his whole life.

Fred Pope smelled like old cigarette smoke and alcohol. The kind that boiled in your gut and permeated from your pores. It alerted everyone to what you did in your spare time.

I could attest to this, as the grumpy man before me had been passed out on the couch most of the times I had seen him. I think he had spoken seven words to me when I dated his son.

"I thought you were a smart girl, Briar." He leaned in as his hot alcohol-soaked breath caressed my skin, and I fought nausea as my stomach rolled.

"Guess not." I did my best to shrug and sound calm.

I wasn't calm. I was fucking terrified. I didn't want to be, but I was scared of Adam and Fred without Morgan as a buffer in the house. Morgan was predictable and still a kid in many ways, and I knew him. These other men were something else altogether.

"A human that willingly has a vampire boyfriend. What kind of sick world are we living in now?"

"I guess one where grown-ass men are kidnapping high school girls, thinking it's justified."

"Still got a mouth on you."

"And you still have halitosis."

"I don't know what that is."

"That tracks."

He screwed his face up as if he were about to spit on me. I wasn't sure that if he did, I could keep the vomit in my stomach. Though I wasn't sure what there was to throw up right now. *Kool-Aid?*

"Adam, take these damn ropes off her legs and arms. Let her take a piss, stand outside the bathroom."

Adam was at his side like a loyal dog waiting to be called. He eyed me almost hungrily as if he were going to enjoy following me to the bathroom, and a slight shiver ran through me.

He took the ropes off too slowly, and I realized he was touching my skin more than necessary, almost caressing it with his fingers. My blood ran cold as disgust and anxiety wove through my spine. A lot of women felt unease when in the presence of a threat; it prickled my skin, warning me of danger.

"All right, little viper, let's take it nice and slow. I'll stand outside unless you want me to watch you."

"I've been peeing on my own since I was three; I think I'll manage." My mouth puckered at his insinuation as he led me to the bathroom.

Instead of focusing on his hand on my arm, I tried to think of a way to get out. But as Adam opened the bathroom door, I was dismayed to see it was not more extensive than a closet, and there was no window.

"If you take too long, I'll come anyway." His mouth was on my ear, and I jerked back violently. I thought of trying to hit him, but fear squeezed my chest.

Morgan had told him not to put his hands on me, and I did not doubt that my striking him first would escalate to him breaking his word to his little brother.

I slipped inside the bathroom and shut the door in his face instead. I felt along the wall for a light as the cold air bit into my skin. The lightheadedness of high blood sugar was more present now that I was standing up. My mouth was dry, and I was so thirsty my brain told me I might die if I didn't drink water.

I hiked my dress up and sat on the toilet. I pulled my underwear down, keeping my eye on the door, feeling exposed. The pervert beyond could come in at any moment, so I finished as fast as I could and washed my hands, the icy temperature of the water stinging my hands.

"You done in there?" Adam asked as I opened the door, giving him a sour look.

He didn't hesitate to reach out and grab my arm again, more roughly than before. A knock sounded, echoing in the almost empty house.

"Oh, I hope that's your boyfriend," Adam whispered.

My heart rate increased as I heard Fred somewhere in the house. I held my breath and closed my eyes as Adam moved me back into the living room. I opened my eyes after I heard talking and more footsteps.

A door slammed closed. The kitchen light flicked on.

People approached us, and when they turned the corner, I frowned. Maisie stood next to Fred Pope, dressed like Laura Croft in skinny jeans and a black athletic shirt with a leather harness that held two of Adam and Morgan's strange double-bladed weapons.

"I'm surprised you haven't managed to screw this up." Superiority rang out in her voice. It was laid on even thicker than her typical holier-than-thou attitude.

"Fuck off, Maisie," Adam growled. "What are you doing here? I thought you were a bloodsucker sympathizer."

"My father is more civilized than you are and taught me better manners, to be sure." She looked at her uncle like he was a bag of hot garbage. "But I don't share his views on vampires. Two fewer vampires in Ironside will keep the community safer."

I furrowed my brows and narrowed my eyes at her.

"It's not their fault, but still, the problem should be eradicated." She shrugged one shoulder.

The sting of betrayal was no new feeling for me. But at that moment, I hated Maisie Pope more than anyone alive.

"Aw, you thought we were friends." She mocked me, and I lunged forward.

Caught by surprise, Adam let me go, but Maisie was ready for me with a smile on her lips as she drew one of her weapons. She elbowed me in the stomach with embarrassing ease and threw me to the floor. I gasped as the wind that had been knocked from me as she pressed her blade to my throat. Her face came within inches of mine with a shit-eating grin.

She winked at me, and my emotions went for another roller coaster loop. It wasn't a malicious gesture but a playful one where I saw the Maisie I knew underneath.

"We are going to check your car," Fred announced. "No offense intended, of course, but this is the first time I've heard of you holding to the old ways."

"Go ahead, and I'll watch her." She stood up and jutted her chin to the door where Adam and Fred exited.

When they had gone, she held her hand out to me, where I was still lying on the ground, staring up at her; trepidation marred my reaction.

"Sorry about that." Her hand was still extended as I accepted it and stood up.

As soon as I regained my balance, I punched her in the stomach, and she grunted.

"No problem." I smiled as she scowled, sheathing her blade.

Chapter Thirty-Seven

Darcy

Crispin and I crouched in the brush at the back of the house. As far as safehouses went, it was relatively hidden. The only access point was surrounded by dense evergreen trees and brush by a long dirt road.

Maisie had instructed us to get out along the main road and follow the river in. From there, she gave us several instructions like we were in the boy scouts as we looked for large rock markers, and things that led us right where she said they would be. We were staring at the back of the house, primarily hidden in the shrubbery.

"I want an iron-on patch for this," Crispin grumbled what I had been thinking, and despite the situation, I smiled.

We were dressed in dark clothes—Crispin in black jeans, a black hoodie, and me in black joggers and a black crewneck. We both had beanies on like we were about to commit a petty crime. It had taken a good while to walk to the house. Even if we could run a bit faster than humans, it was still tiring, so we opted to conserve our energy. The sun was not up. Crispin's nose was red from the biting air, and I had no doubt mine looked similar.

"Hey," Crispin said to me in a hushed whisper.

I turned to him in response.

"I love you."

I frowned and whispered back, "I love you too. Are you dying of cancer or something?"

"Not that I'm aware of." He smiled, and we left it at that.

It lessened the tension in the air and relaxed me a bit as we waited in the cold to save my girlfriend.

Crispin's phone vibrated in his pocket, and my heart leaped in my chest.

He tipped the screen so I could see the screen.

Maisie: Come on in, boys.

He nodded to me as he slipped his phone back into his pocket. She said she would unlock the door that led into the back bedroom, so we moved out from the brush and kept our eyes out for any psycho vampire hunters. Crispin didn't look as nervous as I was as he reached the door first, and insisted on looking inside before me. He nodded again, and I took a deep breath as he flung it open wide and entered the house with me at his heels.

We made it through the door that dumped into a pretty bare room, and as my eyes scanned the area, they landed on Briar, who was tied to a chair in front of a TV.

Her stare was panicked, and then relaxed as she smiled at me.

"Two vampires entering a house they weren't invited into." The man I assumed was Mr. Pope walked into the room's doorway. "You know what we do to trespassers?" he asked low and threatening, and to be honest, I felt a little threatened.

Vampires were stronger and faster than humans, but hunters were trained to track and kill us. So, while Crispin and I were stronger...we had not been preparing our entire lives for a fight to the death.

"We kill them," another guy said, sidling up to the older man. He looked like Morgan, only older, with more hatred in his eyes.

His gaze shifted between my brother and me as I saw that raw hatred on display. He did hate us for what we were—raised to hate something unfamiliar.

"They aren't trespassing." Maisie's voice came from behind us from the doorway of a bedroom. "I invited them. My dad's name is on the deed to the house, after all. I have as much familial right to invite them as you do."

I watched the two men's expressions flicker through so many different things but again land on hatred, only now it was focused on Maisie.

"Traitor, you'd choose a leech over your own family?" the younger man asked.

"All day." She came forward with words sure and steady. "If the choice is a family that values vampire lives below their own because of a disease, then yes, I'll choose them."

"You're going to regret that," the older man said.

"No, I don't think so. It's three against two." Maisie paused and nodded to Briar, who stood up, dropping some rope behind her chair. "Three and a half."

Briar scowled at her.

"We don't want to fight. We want to take Briar and leave peacefully." I interrupted to de-escalate the situation.

"So, you can go on terrorizing our town?" the younger one asked.

"Define terrorize. Us being alive is threatening to humanity?" Crispin asked.

"Who knows when you will snap and go on a killing spree? Your instincts could give way at any moment. Your kind can't help it. It's genetics. No matter how hard you try or what you claim, you are nothing more than your baser urges," the older man explained to us as if we were in grade school and he was trying to explain something to a child. Anger flared in the pit of my stomach, but I clamped my mouth shut.

Both men pulled blades from their belts as my heart rate increased.

"Uncle Fred, Adam. It doesn't have to go like this," Maisie warned.

All I could think was that I was damn glad I had decided to text Mom and Dad outside. They would no doubt be driving here in a blind panic, and I would deal with the repercussions of the lies I had told later. But we needed them, and playing teenage vampire heroes was not the right choice.

When I looked up again, the dad lunged forward. But Maisie stepped forward to meet him, and his blade met hers with a metal-to-metal sound.

"Don't do this, girl," he said as they grappled for a second.

Crispin was warily looking at Adam, who was staring at us with a sort of hunger that worried me. We were all frozen at that moment as someone came through the front door. Morgan turned the corner with wide eyes surveying the situation.

Fred knocked Maisie in the face with his elbow as she reeled back and grounded herself again with her blade up to protect her face. Crispin let out what I could only describe as a growl looking in Fred's direction.

Adam took advantage of the distraction and lunged for Crispin. Without thinking, I stepped in front of him. I had no weapon or defense against him. I had no plan, only to stop him from getting to Crispin.

I grabbed one of his arms and attempted to twist him away. He yowled in pain, and I cringed, worried I had broken it. He jerked the hand down with the blade down to arc toward my face. I let go of his arm to cover my face and push him back.

He stumbled back and fell to the floor with the force of my push.

"Hey," Morgan said, and Crispin was on him before I could say anything.

I watched in slight horror as Crispin pinned him to the wall, his eyes red, and fangs bared. He ripped into Morgan's throat, and the hunter cried out. Crispin bit his wrist. I could only stare, shocked, as he brought his wrist, now dripping blood, up to Morgan's throat.

"How would you like to become what you hate most?" His voice was not his own. It was raw and angry. It was the voice of a vampire who had entirely given over.

"Crispin," I yelled at him.

"No, please," Fred cried out from the floor where Maisie and Briar had knocked him down. She was above his head with an empty syringe in one hand, and Briar was sitting on top of him.

What the hell did Maisie have a syringe for, and what was in it?

"I wonder what your family would say then? Would they shun you? Would you have to seek help from the people you hunt?"

"Crispin, please." The voice was soft, and it came from Maisie. "Don't."

I nearly thanked her as Crispin's posture softened. And he pulled his wrist a little further away. His eyes met hers across the room. I felt my fangs come down, and I had no doubt my eyes were red with adrenaline, but I tried to take a few steadying breaths.

Then, just as I started to think we might make it out of this okay, eyes solely on Crispin, I felt a sharp bite of pain in my abdomen.

I stumbled back. I was gasping for breath.

Adam removed his blade from my stomach, eyes filled with a joyful lust.

Chapter Thirty-Eight

Briar

He fell back, and I heard a scream loose from my lips. He grabbed his abdomen. Crispin was nearly so quick I didn't see him. He grabbed Adam by his hair with a growl, smashed his head into the wall, and the hunter fell unconscious to the floor. Maisie had injected her uncle with something, and his head now lolled to the side, his eyes half closed. The two vampire hunters were incapacitated, but my eyes were on Darcy, whose eyes were wide, looking down at his bloody hands. I scrambled up off the floor.

His eyes had gone back to regular blue, and he stared over at me as I hurried over to him as he started to fall. He was taller and heavier than me, but I did my best to set him down gently.

"Darcy, Darcy," Crispin said, and I was surprised to find that he had tears streaming down his cheeks. "Mom and dad will be here soon. It's going to be fine. He'll be fine; his body will heal it." He sounded like he was trying to convince himself.

Morgan stood where he had been with Crispin watching the entire scene unfold. He didn't move; only held his hand to his throat.

"If you so much as move, I'll kill you myself." Maisie threatened Morgan. "What can we do?" she asked, the edge of panic in her voice.

"He needs blood, Crispin said, not mine; it won't work. The silver will slow his body from healing the wound, but if he can get fresh blood, he'll make it."

Darcy's eyes were glazed over as he stared at the wall. He stared at nothing like someone already half gone, slumped over; his muscles had given up. He was breathing heavily.

"I can," Maisie said, her voice violently fragile. She didn't want to. Even as everything around me felt like I was in a fishbowl, I could tell she didn't want to.

"No." I moved so I was sitting between Darcy's legs. "I'll do it; you go flag down their parents."

Maisie nodded and ran out of the house like she was being chased.

"Crispin, will you hold him up?" I asked, and Crispin moved to hold his shoulders steady.

I was sitting with my back against his chest. For some reason, what I was about to do felt intimate, and I felt a little strange to have Crispin sitting there about to watch. Of course, that was ridiculous. This was to save Darcy. There was nothing romantic about it at all.

"Hey, Darcy, keep your eyes open, okay? Keep them open," I said, as I peered up and back at his face, which was now slick with sweat. His skin felt feverish as it radiated a warmth that I could feel. that we were so close. His eyes slid to mine like a dream, slowly as if he hadn't a care in the entire world.

"It's alright, buddy, just hold on," Crispin assured.

"Where's the best place?" I hated the shakiness in my voice. I hated that I was scared for myself.

"You don't have to do this." Crispin reached around to put a hand on my shoulder.

"Yes, I do."

"Your neck, if you can stand it, or your wrist."

I leaned my head back on Darcy's shoulder and panicked a little that his eyes had closed fully. I pulled his head down to my exposed throat.

"Hey Darcy, you gotta drink, okay?"

"No." His voice came out stronger than I thought it would.

"Yes," I argued with him.

His mouth grazed my skin, and I shivered.

"I'm here, Darcy. I'll make sure you don't hurt her. You have to. You won't make it; you're losing too much blood."

"If you die, I'll kill you, asshole," I said to him, and he started to chuckle silently, and the laugh turned into a cough.

"Come on. I don't want to have to find another boyfriend. It's too much work." I pushed his head a bit, so his mouth was against my skin, and I felt the graze of his teeth. "Please, Darcy. Please," I begged, and I felt tears spill over the rim of my eyes.

I yelped a little as I felt a sharp bite of pain on my neck. However, as soon as I thought it, it was gone. The sharpness was replaced with overwhelming warmth and euphoria. A sensation of pleasure flooded everything else, and I couldn't remember why I had been crying for the life of me. I couldn't remember why I had been scared. Who would fear pure pleasure? My heart sang, and I heard myself moaning as if I were listening from outside myself.

Darcy's arm wrapped around my waist as I leaned back into him, closing my eyes, completely content to let him drink me dry. I might even beg him to. If he stopped drinking my blood, I felt as if I might die. I had never experienced any feeling like this before. At that moment, I belonged to Darcy Booker in a way I had never belonged to anyone.

I felt him straighten; I could feel him regain his strength, and my brain told me he would stop and pull away. So, I held his head to my neck, whimpering at the thought.

"Okay," I heard Crispin far away. "You gotta stop, Darcy."

It was instant, like cold water to the face. His pulling away from me felt like abandonment.

"No," I pleaded.

"It's okay." His voice was surer. "It will pass. I've got you."

I curled into him as I shivered from the loss of contact. I felt drowsy and disoriented. Even as the front door opened and I heard panicked adult voices. Everyone was yelling, but I closed my eyes against Darcy's chest, not giving a rat's ass what they were so upset about.

"Don't sleep." His voice was in my ear.

"Don't tell me what to do."

"Wake up, Briar." But I didn't want to.

Maybe the euphoria of being bitten would give way to a lovely dream where Darcy still had his mouth on me.

"Look at me, Sunshine."

My eyes opened to meet his peering down at me. I cringed at the pain that was still present in them, but they were open. Open and looking into mine with concern, and as long as they were open, I could do whatever he asked

"I'm not the one who got themselves stabbed," I mumbled.

"I'm sorry to have inconvenienced you while saving your ass from your crazy ex."

"I wouldn't be in danger if I wasn't in love with a vampire. Speaking of, how do I taste?"

I looked up at him, and in the light streaming in from the windows, I watched him color and turn away shyly.

"Too sweet. Let's get you some insulin."

Chapter Thirty-Nine

Darcy

The doctor that visited houses of vampires in this area was Dr. Shodu, but she told me I could call her Charlot. She was a tall and slender woman with brown skin and shiny black hair that was pulling back and away from her face to tie back in a quick braid. She had been to our house a handful of times in the last week, and she had been as put together then as she was now. She wore a long shimmering blue dress and heels that might have made her as tall as my dad. She pulled back the covers, and I was a little self-conscious without a shirt in front of her.

Of course, that was ridiculous; she was a doctor. She'd seen more than a teenage vampire with no shirt on. Though she seemed to sense my discomfort, the smile which had once seemed pleasant turned slightly amused.

"I'm going to check the wound," she said, and I tried not to wince as she removed the bandages covering the place where I had gotten stabbed.

Hardly any evidence remained. It would scar, and the sutures she had put in two days ago seemed a little red and irritated still. I guessed it would be a faint pink line by the end of the day.

"Looks good, Darcy," she said, pressing the bandage back into place. "You can take a shower tonight if you wish. Please keep it clean, but you should be all good to go. Drink a lot of blood today and rest."

"Can I play basketball with my friends tomorrow?"

"Yes, you'll be well enough by then."

"Thank you." I pulled the cover back over me, and she nodded.

"I'll tell your parents on my way out. You were a very compliant patient."

"It's easy to be when I heal three hundred times faster than a normal person."

"That is true." She gave me a smile like an adult who doesn't know what else to say to a kid.

"Thanks." I waved to her and picked up my laptop to finish choosing my classes for my first year of undergrad.

Luckily the week before prom was the last week of school for seniors, so I hadn't missed any classes on Monday or Tuesday due to my injury. I just needed to make it to graduation in two weeks, and then it was summer—the last summer before college. Briar would call me an idiot, but it felt different to think of it. This would be the last time I would be a kid. I wanted to make the most of it, and take Briar everywhere with me. Maybe go on a couple of day road trips with Crispin.

Thinking of my brother brought a small bout of concern. On Monday morning, OOVA came to our house for their bi-yearly inspection. We had our family meeting on the couch downstairs as the man named Mr. Roperal talked a little about the predicament from the day before. He assured us that The League of Hunters was dealing with the Pope family very severely. Adam and the dad were going to serve time for kidnapping, and Morgan was put on probation.

He had given Crispin and me very unpleasant looks the entire time as if he knew that we had been less than honest. I felt guilty, but my brother had looked pleased as punch.

Then at the end of the meeting, when we had gotten up, Mr. Roperal had asked Crispin and my parents to stay. My dad had given me a look that said I needed to go away. When I questioned Crispin about it later, he was all defensive and quiet. I knew better than to pry, so I let it drop. The slight worry still ate at me. Maybe I would try to talk to him again before tonight and make sure he was okay.

"Hey, Sport." My dad's voice came from my doorway, and the other shoe I had been waiting for came crashing down.

"What's up, Dad?"

"Well, I thought we could have our little chat now." He invited himself in and sat on the end of my bed. Which was fair as he paid the mortgage on the house, my room being a part of the house. I suppose he had the right.

"I think you have been more than generous by giving me the last couple of days and not coming to collect on it."

"I'm so glad we agree about how generous I've been." I winced a little as his voice held a hard edge to it. I had been expecting an edge, but it stung a little all the same. "You want me to get your mom? I told her I could probably handle it, but if you'd rather have her here...."

"No, that's okay; I think you can just give her the summary."

"You got it."

It was silent after that, with each of us hesitating on the edge of the start. I didn't know if I should launch into an explanation or wait for him to ask a question. In the past, it seemed that whenever I would launch into an explanation, I fumbled it. Somehow I ended up in more trouble than I had been in before. So I waited for him to say something.

"Well, I guess I'll start," he said finally. "What the actual fuck Darcy Kenton Booker?"

I was surprised that Dad used my full name; that was usually Mom's gig. Also, with the swearing, my mom and dad didn't swear unless something was really wrong. Mom, especially Mom, but it was a little concerning with Dad too. *Perfect, off to a rough start already.*

"Well." I rubbed the back of my head and looked up at the ceiling. "I don't know where to start."

"You better figure it out in the next five seconds."

"Well, I started fake dating Briar, Dad, and at first it was just fake, but... it turned into something not so fake really quickly. I know I should have called it off, and then one day, when you and Mom had to drive to get blood that one day we ran out; Crispin and I went to school even though you guys told us to stay home. I shouldn't have gone."

My father's eyes were wide, and his lips were pursed into a line, but he nodded for me to continue.

"Well, Briar's boyfriend was being a jerk to her. You know he's kinda a tool."

"I'm aware of the stock he comes from." He shifted on my bed.

"Yeah, well, I was on edge from being hungry, and I saw him grab her, and I just kinda...." I shrugged.

"You kinda what?"

"I kinda got protective of Briar and told him to get lost. Well, she grabbed me and kinda kissed me."

"Why do you keep saying kinda. You either kiss someone or you don't." The irritation hadn't lessened.

"Okay, well, she did, and I kinda... I mean, I did. I definitely did bite her on her lip a little."

"Okay, and then what?"

"Then I ran into the bathroom, and Crispin came and got me, and we went home."

"Okay." He nodded. "And you didn't tell me and your mom because?"

"I was worried I'd be in trouble."

"You're in trouble for lying, Darcy. Your mom and I know what it's like to be young vampires. There will be accidents and mess-ups. We don't expect you to be perfect."

"Yes, sir."

"Are you sure you didn't tell us because you knew we would tell you that you couldn't see Briar anymore?"

"That may have had a little bit to do with it."

"I have to tell you, kiddo, that you aren't exactly the actor you might think you are. From the first time she had dinner here, your mother and I knew you had feelings for her. I know we might seem stupid."

"I don't think you're stupid."

"You're eighteen, Darcy; I can't very well ground you or take your video game time away like I did when you were little. I just hoped...."

I felt emotion crawling up my throat as I watched my dad's eyes get a little watery. My dad was not a cryer; if he cried, I would surely cry. No one wanted to see two men crying on a bed together.

"I had hoped you would know that you could trust us with this. You have your own life. There will be things you can't tell us. Believe me when I tell you that we don't want to know everything, but I thought you knew that stuff like this; you could have trusted me. I know Crispin struggles with trust, and I understand that part of him, understand why he doesn't...but I thought you would know we would be there for you, Darcy."

"I do know that, Dad." I struggled around the knot in my throat. "That's why I texted you before we went to get Briar. I just, I guess, forgot for a minute."

"That's alright, as long as you know. I know that you are responsible. I truly believe that you would never hurt that girl. I know that at the core of my person, but you know the reason your mom and I are so careful is that you guys have less control right now."

"I know."

"I like Briar."

I looked at him again as my gaze wandered to my hands, which were worrying themselves together.

"I can still see her?"

"Darcy, did you not hear me say you are eighteen? My role in your life has shifted from the warden of your life to advice giver and counselor. I like your girlfriend. I'm just begging you to be careful with her because you don't want to kill someone you love on accident."

The reminder and thought of what was hiding beneath the seemingly average packaging of me chilled me. Flashes of the corpse of Briar filled my mind, and I nearly started sobbing again.

"Tell me what else happened... and what is the deal with the Pope kid?"

So I started where I had left off. Leaving out any details, I assumed he might not want to know. and the nagging anxiety I had felt for the past couple of months began to melt away.

Chapter Forty

Briar

"You wanted to see me, Mrs. Sheridan?"

"You've already passed your classes, Briar. You can call me Jackie."

"Somehow, it's less appealing now that you are giving me permission."

Mrs. Sheridan snorted out a laugh as I leaned against the doorframe of her office. I didn't have school; technically, this was the last day for the juniors, sophomores, and freshmen. I had gotten a call from the office that Mrs. Sheridan had wanted to meet with me. If it had been any other adult in this damned place, I would have said no, but....

"Graduating with honors," she said, rummaging around in a drawer I had never seen her open in all my time in this office. She pulled out a ziplock bag full of vanilla tootsie rolls.

"What else you got in there?" I inquired, stepping forward to peek, unable to squash the curiosity.

She did nothing to hide it. Inside were individual zip-lock bags of all different candies. There must have been at least twenty-five.

"Jackie, what is this?" I looked at the candy jar on her desk, smiling at its emptiness.

"For my repeat offenders."

The realization that she put each student's favorite candy in the jar when they were coming in irritated and impressed me.

"Here I was, thinking I was special."

She handed me the bag of candy and smiled that warm smile that made me feel as seen as I had ever been.

"You are, Briar, just not in the ways that you think."

"My dad said something to me a couple of weeks ago about his role changing in my life, and it sparked the idea for my speech today. It is daunting to leave this parking lot for the last time today. All our roles are changing in a big way, and I think that fear we have is healthy...."

There were so many worries, and Darcy's speech resonated a little too much. I was scared to start new things. In two weeks, I would begin my electrical apprenticeship. Would I be good at it? Was it what I wanted to do? Was I making a mistake by not signing up for college classes? I had no idea, and if I let myself sink into the question spiral, I always felt like life was pointless, and I wanted to take a long nap or punch someone in the face.

I took a deep breath and listened to my boyfriend finish his valedictorian speech in my cap and gown, tapping my rolled diploma against my knee. I was a little pissed that Darcy had graduated with a better GPA than me. Mostly. I was irritated because I had lost a trivial bet, and he had won the right to casually bring up this fact in the next week's conversation. Yesterday we had gotten soft serve at the frosty spot, and he had told the woman who gave us our cones that he had earned a higher GPA than me. So I accidentally dropped my ice cream on his lap when we sat down.

I said he could bring it up; I hadn't said there wouldn't be con-sequences.

Once the caps were thrown, and the cheering had been carried away by the light breeze, we all took pictures with our parents. My mom talked to Mr. and Mrs. Booker.

Nancy, Gunnar, and Zoe came too, and Nancy gave me a half-assed excuse as to why my dad hadn't been able to make it. I wish it didn't bother me, but it did a little. Darcy had given me a sad look, not fooled by the roll of my eyes. I watched as Darcy walked over and talked to Erik and his parents. Suddenly, I caught sight of Kristy looking at me like I was the spawn of Satan from the edge of the bleachers next to her dad.

I waved to her, and then we exchanged middle fingers.

"No love lost there, huh?" Crispin was beside me, and I nearly screeched from surprise.

"You fucking creep." I stepped away from him. "Why are you sneaking up on people."

"I need to ask you something."

"You looking for a new skincare routine, pretty boy? What the hell could you want?"

"I have an excellent skincare routine, thanks."

There was no bite or humor behind his words. Generally, there was a playful snap between us that I enjoyed. Crispin could take sarcasm and razzing better than most people, but now it was flat and distracting. I faced him with an eyebrow raised. Darcy had mentioned that he had been acting weird for the last two weeks. He and Maisie had avoided hanging out with the group, and part of me wondered if something had happened between them.

Trudy, Maisie, Triana, and I were going to have a junk food girls' night tonight, and Maisie had asked at least three times if Crispin was going to be there. Like she wanted to make extra sure he wasn't.

"If you won the lottery tomorrow, what would be the most relieving thing that money could fix for you?"

"What the fuck kinda question is that?" My brows furrowed together.

"Answer the fucking question Grey, please. Try for once in your life not to be a pain in the ass."

"Geez, okay." I thought about it for a moment, but I didn't have to. "I guess that my mom wouldn't have to pay for private health insurance anymore or any of my diabetic supplies."

"Is that very expensive?" He wasn't being an ass. He just sounded curious.

"Very."

"Okay." He walked off, and I didn't have the energy to yell at him to tell him what an absolute weirdo he was.

"Hey baby, I gotta go to work," my mom said, walking up to me with her arms outstretched, and I embraced her. "I am so proud of you."

"Thanks, Mom. I graduated the mandated amount of school required from a human."

"And with such a lovely boyfriend," Mom said, nodding to Darcy, who had come to stand next to us.

"Eh, mediocre at best." I shrugged.

"Mediocre; look at me. I'm charming and adorable," he said, giving my mom a side hug.

I couldn't argue. I wanted to, but I just scoffed at him instead.

Yesterday after the ice cream incident, he took me home. I kissed him goodbye, and our kisses had turned into a little more, as much as a little more can be across a consul in a car. When he pulled away, he seemed so nervous. He had loudly blurted out that he couldn't have sex with me. I'd nearly peed my pants laughing as he looked at me in disapproval.

"It's not that I don't want to Briar, or I haven't thought about it. I need more time to make sure I've got a handle on my...vampire stuff. I totally get it if you..."

He started to say before I kissed him again and got out of his car.

I didn't think I was ready to have sex anyway. However, the thought of being with Darcy like that wasn't anxiety-inducing as it had been with Morgan. If there was any boy on the planet who I would be okay with being my first, it was Darcy. I would rather die than tell him that, so I kept it to myself and laughed at him instead.

"You have fun with your girls tonight," Mom said, kissing me on the cheek before leaving.

"You hungry?" We started walking toward the exit of the football field where the ceremony had been held.

"More ice cream?" I asked him as he slipped his hand into mine.

"Maybe something less...cold."

"Coffee?"

"How about a beverage at room temperature?"

"Ah, my favorite thing to drink. Room temperature things."

"You know what my favorite thing is to drink?"

He stopped and pushed me against the chain link fence, gently bending low to kiss me. His mouth worked over mine as I realized we had become one of those obnoxious teenage couples that kissed in public. I couldn't bring myself to care that much at that moment.

"The blood of a girl a little less smart than me."

I punched him in the stomach, and he stumbled back as a bubble of laughter left him. He fell back on his back dramatically, laughing away at my expense. His hands were resting under his head as he looked at me, his laughter subsiding.

"I hate you, Booker."

"I love you too, Sunshine."

Epilogue

Maisie

"Before we start, Crispin and I need to tell you something," I said, and Trudy looked up at me from where she was putting on her bowling shoes.

Briar already had hers on and would no doubt murder the opposite team of whichever she was assigned. Boys versus girls was always popular, which suited me just fine.

"Does it have to do with the fact that you two have been downright cordial to each other since we got here?" Briar piped up, and I shot her a harsh glare.

"I said, let's not do it before the game." Crispin let out a heavy sigh as if he were already sick of me. "Don't you remember when I said that to you?"

I need a cigarette.

"I try not to remember anything you say to me." I bit my tongue, cursing myself as Crispin gave me a closed-lipped smile raising his eyebrows.

Anger surged in my stomach, and I swallowed the words I always had reserved for him. I thought it would make the news worse if we did our regular bickering before I delivered it. Even if the day before, Crispin had accused me of not being able to get through this without snapping at him. He had just proved his point, and

I wanted to stick him with a hunter blade, but the bowling alley might not be the place.

I needed to make this as easy to digest for Trudy as possible. I knew she was going to balk. Hell, I knew she would light me up as soon as we were alone. I hadn't even gotten my story straight. What was I going to tell her? What story could I weave to make her believe that Crispin and I were in love? It was nearly impossible to think of one.

Darcy looked at me encouragingly, which meant he already knew. Of course, he did. Stupid Crispin couldn't leave his mouth shut. I smiled at Darcy, however. It would be one thousand percent easier to announce if he was the Booker brother I was about to be entangled with for the next five years. He was so kind and understanding; his brother, on the other hand...an absolute pain in my ass.

"Crispin and I...." I struggled as the words got caught in my throat. I felt too warm for the temperature of the room. I was aware I looked like an idiot and hated to look like an idiot.

"Maisie and I are getting married in September," Crispin said with no feeling or emotion to be heard in his voice. Of course, there was none; he was just as opposed to this as I was. But we had both been given a choice, and there was no backing out.

"Are you pregnant?" Briar's voice came to me, and I gave her an open-mouthed stare.

"Come on, Briar, do I look like the kinda guy who doesn't know how to wrap it up?" Crispin laughed, and I turned my incredulous expression on him.

How could he be laughing right now?

"You want me to answer that?" she responded.

"I'm sorry, back the hell up? Is this some sort of joke? If so, please tell me to laugh," Trudy interjected, and I closed my eyes before turning to her.

I faced precisely what I had been afraid of. The eyes of my best friend filled with an angry sort of hurt. Of course, this was out of left field and I hadn't told her anything. I hadn't even known what to say.

Hey Tru, you know Crispin, whom I hate with a burning passion? Yeah, that Crispin. We are getting married in a couple of months and traveling the country to be the face of the peace treaty between OOVA and the LOH. Want to be my maid of honor?

I knew it was terrible as I held her gaze; I could only silently plead with her to understand something I would most likely never be able to explain. Her hurt was what I worried about the most, but I would be lying if I said the thought of what other people would think didn't plague me from time to time. The other kids from our high school and our family didn't know about us being hunters. There would be so much judgment from so many sides, and it felt like it was crushing me. The perfect preppy princess getting married at eighteen. While I always tried to give off an air of uncaring. I cared a lot more than people could know.

They would assume I had gotten pregnant, or worse, that I was in some stupid puppy love and had just married the first guy that had called me pretty. I glared at Crispin, though not his fault; my irritation had to fall somewhere.

"Married married? Like in holy matrimony?" Erik sounded horrified. "You don't get along at all... let alone...."

He didn't finish what all the rest of us were thinking. Let alone love each other.

No, we didn't love each other, and the thought of being married to Crispin and spending the next year attending functions together, forced to act as if we were sick in love, made me nauseous. But it would be worth it. I told myself for the hundredth time since that day after we rescued Briar from the Pope family. I said it like a prayer every night while I lay in bed.

"What the hell?" Trudy said again, swiveling her head to look at everyone. Like she was missing something.

"Yeah, married," I said, taking a breath and running my hand over my face.

"For better or for worse?" Briar asked.

"For richer or for poorer," Crispin responded.

"In sickness and health," Erik said, eyes wide at the strange exchange.

For as long as we both shall live.

But I didn't have the stomach to say it.

Too Sweet Playlist

Kiss It — Dorothy
Sugar — Maroon Five
BITE — Troye Sivan
Starving — Hailee Steinfeld, Grey, Zedd
Good 4 u — Olivia Rodrigo
Pushing — Andy Grammer
I Can't Help — Shoffy, Sarcastic Sounds
Disease — Matchbox Twenty
Here Come Those Eyes — Chris Rice
Maniac — Conan Gray
Maybe Don't(feat. JP Saxe) — Maisie Peters, JP Saxe
Deal With It (feat. Kellis) —Ashnikko, Kellis
IM NOT SORRY — Royal and the Serpent
Teenage Dream — Stephen Dawes
Girlfriend — Charlie Puth
Bullet With Butterfly Wings — Violet Orlandi
Push it — Salt N' Pepa
Home — ZZ Ward

Author Notes and Acknowledgments

I feel like this section will be longer than any I've ever done.

This book is so dear to my heart because I was diagnosed with type one diabetes at twenty, just months before my twenty-first birthday. The diagnosis changed my life forever. I struggle with this autoimmune disease daily, from being conscious of everything I eat to worrying about the financials of purchasing insulin and sensors. Briar's story poured out of me, and often I cried with her. I know those who also battle with this will understand, and all I hoped to do was to bring you a story that might make you laugh a little.

Things could be worse, there are much worse things to be diagnosed with than Type One Diabetes, but that does not mean your struggle isn't worth expressing. I see you, and I know how hard you fight to control your sugar. More importantly, Briar and I know that some days you just can't do it anymore, and you're tired; that's okay too.

You are so strong, and I'm proud of you.

Thank you to my Lord and Savior, who has allowed this part of my life to help and lift others. There is good in this shitty diagnosis.

To my sister, who, when I told her that I was going to write a diabetic book, assumed I meant a self-help book said, "I don't think you're qualified." Thank you for that. I think about it once a week and laugh.

To my husband, who has always been so supportive of my dream to be an author. I love you, Barrett. Thank you for supporting my insulin addiction.

To Brittany, Shaelby R., Syndie S., Meagan S., Jonathan M., and my exceptional practitioners, every single one of you, in some way, has made me feel less alone on this diabetic journey.

My Alpha readers Willow, Briah, and Emma, the encouragement of early readers fuels me and you helped shape this story. My beta readers and my ARC readers, you are all so important to each step of the process, and I appreciate every single one of you. My editor Reanna, and my talented cover designer, thank you for making me look more incredible than I am.

And, as always, to you, reader, I cannot weave these tales without you.

About the Author

Author Monroe Wildrose has been stuck between the pages of books since the fifth grade when her father bought her a copy of Eragon by Christopher Paloni. When she's not reading or writing, she can almost always be found with a cup of coffee in her hand as she enjoys time with those she adores. She makes her home at the base of the Sierra Nevada Mountains where she and the loves of her life, her husband and two rowdy toddlers, are fortunate enough to have Lake Tahoe at their fingertips.

9 798218 115562